RYANN FLETCHER

Christmas, Pursued by a Bear

This novel is entirely a work of fiction. The names, characters and incidents portrayed in it are the work of the author's imagination. Any resemblance to actual persons, living or dead, events or localities is entirely coincidental.

First edition

ISBN: 978-1-9163750-6-2

This book was professionally typeset on Reedsy.
Find out more at reedsy.com

To all the women who want to be Bears. Roar loud, and scare the neighbors.

Contents

CHAPTER ONE   1

CHAPTER TWO   13

CHAPTER THREE   22

CHAPTER FOUR   31

CHAPTER FIVE   35

CHAPTER SIX   41

CHAPTER SEVEN   53

CHAPTER EIGHT   65

CHAPTER NINE   74

CHAPTER TEN   84

CHAPTER ELEVEN   90

CHAPTER TWELVE   95

CHAPTER THIRTEEN   100

CHAPTER FOURTEEN   110

CHAPTER FIFTEEN   116

CHAPTER SIXTEEN   125

CHAPTER SEVENTEEN   138

Epilogue   151

About the Author   153

Also by Ryann Fletcher   154

CHAPTER ONE

Andie gave the last tent peg a final smack with the mallet and sat back on her haunches to admire her work. Finally, some peace and quiet. A chance to get some real shots in, maybe one good enough to submit to the wildlife photography of the year competition. The clouds overhead were threatening rain, and her leaky tent wouldn't last in a big Midwest storm. She shivered in the cold November air and pulled her hoodie tighter around herself. Freezing rain wasn't a good recipe for the perfect photo.

The sun was about an hour from setting, if the app on her phone was right, and she sure as hell didn't want to be out wandering in the dark this far off the path. She wasn't technically supposed to be camping here, not with the public pitches near the front of the reserve, but they were all crammed full. It used to be rare to see any campers this time of year in their local county's park, but some goddamned website that aggregates the most picturesque places for Instagram influencer photos had drawn them all here in droves, packing the reserve weekend after weekend, many of them unaccustomed to camping, leaving their crap everywhere.

She hooked a flashlight to the carabiner on her belt loop and slung her camera bag over her shoulder. Even though it was unlikely she would have time to set up a tripod for a long exposure shot, she never was quite able to leave parts of her equipment behind. Besides, if someone stumbled on her trespassing tent, she couldn't risk her gear being taken. It would cost her at least a month's salary to replace the lenses alone.

Her worn-in hiking boots scraped softly against the wet leaves, damp from the frigid autumn rain. She climbed over the rusty fence with the No Trespassing sign and spun around to memorize the location. Big birch tree, jagged stump, mushroom ring. She knew better than to go too far this close to sundown, but she only had the weekend to get the perfect photo, the one that would put her pictures in front of the people that matter, and catapult her from the painfully repetitive business of product photography, that soulless, mind-numbing job that made her hate her camera, some days.

The phone in her pocket buzzed weakly. It was on its last legs, too - but she'd put off upgrading in favor of getting a new set of lens filters, instead. She hoped it would be a text from one of her best friends, Mercy or Parker, but it was a reminder that her gas bill was due. Annoyed, she set it to silent and shoved it back in her pocket. She wished she'd known that going paperless meant they'd always be harassing you for money, even before it was time to pay. Between the check engine light on in her old car, and her laptop on its last legs, she could really use a win.

She stepped through a hedge of thick bushes into a small clearing, where the waning light was illuminating the dust particles in the air. Reaching for her camera, she hesitated. Dust wasn't going to win a competition, and she couldn't be wasting time on meaningless pretty shots, not when talented photographers were a dime a dozen. Andie waited, straining her ears to listen for signs of some wildlife. Hell, she might even settle for a raccoon or an impressive buck. It wouldn't be enough, though - last year's winner was a wolf on a ledge, howling at the biggest blue moon she'd ever seen.

The trees shot into the rapidly darkening sky, all but bare now that the weather had turned. The leaves that once graced their branches were crunching under her feet, layers and layers of yellow, orange, and fiery red foliage. Even an owl would be nice. Or a red-tailed hawk, sometimes they frequented this area, though it was getting too dark to get a good snap of one in flight, despite the cool glow of the full moon overhead.

Blowing out a frustrated sigh, she squinted into the growing darkness. The app wasn't wrong about the time of sunset, but the dense forest filtered out more light than she'd hoped. Hell, even just a few weeks back, she would have had almost a whole extra hour to get photos before heading back to camp.

If this weekend was a bust, she might not have many more opportunities to get the perfect photo. Winter was on its way, and deep snow wasn't ideal for camping - besides, it was harder to sneak around when you were leaving footprints all over the place.

Andie turned to leave, and heard rustling behind her. A big rustle, like something taller than a five-point buck. She reached for her camera pack but the tail of the strap got snagged on the flashlight hanging at her hip. "Come on, goddamnit!" she hissed, yanking at the zipper. The bag flew open, sending her camera sailing into a pile of leaves. She scrabbled through the undergrowth, scraping her ungloved hands against hidden thorns. Her fingers brushed against glass and she pulled the camera from the brush triumphantly, and turned to see what her subject was.

A huge, scruffy, pissed off grizzly bear was staring her down.

Thoughts raced through her mind. What the hell were you supposed to do when faced with a bear? Run? No, it would catch her. Climb? Wasn't there a type of bear that could climb? Was it a grizzly? The bear roared so loud, it echoed through the empty woods. Her racing heart was in her throat, and blood pounded in her ears. This was how she would die. Mauled by a bear.

She raised the camera to her eye and snapped once, twice, three times. It was too dark, the settings were all wrong, and she knew it. The bear stepped back and looked at her with an almost quizzical expression, before roaring again, rising up on its hind legs.

Andie ran as fast as her legs would carry her.

* * *

She crashed into the fence, sending herself flying headfirst over the waist high rusted iron into the wet leaves on the other side. She reached for her camera - gone. Andie bit back a sob of frustration at the loss of her camera, the way she paid rent and the only one she had, after trading her old one in for store credit. Whipping out her phone, she searched for ways to deter bears. She couldn't pack up and leave, not with her camera out there somewhere.

"Fire," she whispered, shoving her phone, with its cracked screen, back into the pocket of her hiking pants and zipped it in. She didn't want to lose anything else on this cursed weekend trip. It was supposed to be an opportunity to get the photo of the year, but she'd blown her chance. What in the hell was a damn grizzly bear doing in the Midwest, anyway?

She snatched the flint striker from her pack and scraped sparks into the waiting tinder in her fire pit, bordered with rocks. She hadn't put it there, so it was obvious she wasn't the only one camping in prohibited areas of the reserve. Probably more influencers, maybe even headed for that clearing she'd seen the bear in. It would be pretty at sunrise. Fire caught the dried out pine needles and thin twigs, devouring the kindling and licking at the larger logs. It was lucky that the threatening rain had held off, or she'd be spending the night in her tent, shivering half from the cold, and half from fear that a bear was about to eat her for a midnight snack.

The fire roaring now, she set her foil pack of vegetables and chicken atop the grate and sat back on the log near the edge of the fire pit. As it turned out, running from a bear made someone hungry. The aroma of the food filled the air, and the realization that her camera might be lost forever sank in her gut. She'd have to make her way back to that clearing at first light. The bear would have moved on by then, wouldn't it?

Curious about the bear, Andie pulled her phone out again. Grizzlies shouldn't be in the area, not for thousands of miles, so what was it doing here? She scrolled through her news feeds, looking for news of a zoo breakout, but found nothing. Probably a private exotic animal collector, then - someone who thought a baby cub was cute, and quickly became overwhelmed by the immense size. Should she report the bear to the park ranger on her way out of the park, hopefully after finding her camera? Even if it was water damaged, she could get it repaired.

The thought of the bills piling up on her counter at home made her grimace. Money was going to be tight this month, and even more so if she had to back out of her contract work if her camera was broken or permanently missing. Andie cursed herself under her breath. What a wasted opportunity. No wonder she was still taking boring pictures of boring crap people wanted to list on eBay for more boring people to buy. Wooden picture frames, plain white coffee cups, fake houseplants in matching concrete planters. She did photograph a salt and pepper set shaped like wolves, once.

A rustle near the fence froze her in her seat. The bear. Panic flooded into every muscle and she willed her legs to lift her off the log and start running, but it was like something inside of her was pinning her to the bark, unable to move. With trembling hands, she reached for the pepper spray she always took on trips by herself. It wasn't bear spray, but it might buy her time. Or it might piss off the bear even more.

"You're not supposed to be here," a delicate soprano voice said softly, as a woman swung her leg over the fence.

"Oh my God, I thought you were a bear," Andie said, relieved.

"A bear?" the woman snorted. "No bears around here."

Feeling returned to Andie's legs, and she stood. "No, really, there was a bear in a clearing not far from here, you must have heard—"

"Are you feeling okay? Did you eat some weird mushrooms, or something?"

"What? No, I—"

The woman approached the fire, her red plaid shirt peeking out from under a thick black hoodie. "Sometimes people eat weird shit out here, you find them tripping out, claiming they saw Jesus, or their inner galaxy wolf." She laughed. "Or a bear."

"No, I swear! It scared me so much I dropped my camera, I came running back here to start a fire to try to keep it away."

The woman laughed again. "And you immediately started cooking food, because everyone knows bears *hate* food, right?"

"Oh..." Andie mumbled. The woman was right. She was stupid, cooking up food that would draw any bears straight to her tent. "I didn't think about that. I was hungry, and I guess I thought the campfire would be enough to keep it away from my campsite."

"*My* campsite, actually," the woman said, sitting on the opposite log. "Who do you think built this fire pit?"

A blush crept up Andie's neck. "Oh, I'm so sorry, I didn't see a tent..."

"It's fine."

"I can move if you want me to."

"Nah."

The tense silence was heavy in the air, but the warm glow of the fire showed off the woman's high cheekbones and petite figure, a beautiful face in stark contrast with her torn up hoodie and muddy hiking boots. She looked like she should be on a glossy magazine cover, not traipsing through the woods in the dark.

"Did you... um... should I... do you want some of my dinner?" Andie offered.

"Yeah, that would be great, actually."

"I'm Andie," she said, tossing the next day's foil pack on the fire. She'd worry about tomorrow's dinner later.

"Cat."

"Nice to meet you."

"Yeah."

"Do you live here?"

"No. Some folks do, but I don't." Cat shifted, stretching her legs out in front of her. "You better not rat those people out to the park ranger, by the way. Just leave them alone."

"I'm hardly about to narc on illegal reserve camping, given I literally climbed over a 'No Trespassing' sign to set up here."

"Fucking rangers," Cat grumbled. "They stomp around out here, disturbing all the wildlife, telling people like you and me we can't camp in the forest, public land, meanwhile the pitches are packed full of assholes who can't manage to throw their garbage away, but no one ever says a damn thing to them."

"I know, right? It's nuts. Here I am just trying to do my job, and I'm debating if I should even bother reporting seeing a bear to the ranger because I know they'll get pissy that I was even camping this far off the trail."

Cat eyed her suspiciously. "You're not with the hunting and fishing department, are you?"

"No, I'm a wildlife photographer." That wasn't strictly true, not yet anyway.

"Did you get any pictures of the bear?"

Andie shook her head. "Too dark. Besides, I dropped my camera, I don't even know if I'll be able to find it."

6

"Not even, say, a blurry outline? Nothing that might prove there's a bear out here?"

"I'd have to look at the SD card, but no, probably not."

Cat took one of the foil packs off the fire with a large stick and plopped it into the dirt to cool. "That's a shame about your camera."

"Yeah, if I can't find it, I'm screwed. I have contract work next week to photograph some shelving, and if I can't find it, or it's broken, it's gonna be hard to make rent this month."

"Shelving? I thought you were a wildlife photographer."

Busted, Andie thought. "Well, more of an aspiring one, I guess."

"Yeah, I was wondering what the hell a wildlife photographer was doing in a Midwest park reserve, and not, you know, out in Yellowstone, or up in Denali, or something." Cat smirked. "You might find some *actual* bears in those parks."

"It's so expensive to travel when you're not being sponsored, or you don't know if you'll be able to sell the pictures." Andie sighed. "Truth is, I'm kind of a nobody."

"Aren't we all? Anyway, I couldn't name a single wildlife photographer. Who knows, maybe you accidentally got an amazing shot of that imaginary bear you saw."

"I did see a bear!"

"Maybe we'll get lucky, and it will go eat all the jerks having a rave in the parking lot." Cat picked up the foil pack and peeled it open. "Funny how the rangers never do anything about *that*."

"You really don't like park rangers, do you?"

Cat scowled, her mouth full of food. "No."

"What are you, some kind of... anti-government libertarian?"

"No."

"Well, what then?"

"Let's just say there are no current or future political parties that would represent the issues that most affect me."

"What kind of issues?" Andie pressed, her years in student government coming back to haunt her.

"Didn't anyone ever teach you it's rude to talk politics?"

"I just feel like its something that affects all of us."

Cat crumpled up the now empty foil and set it into the zipped trash bag tied to the supply pack. "What next, are you going to grill me about religion, too? Is this how you make all your friends?"

"Sorry," Andie mumbled. She didn't really have many friends to speak of, and maybe this was why. "Just curious."

"Are you going to eat that?" Cat asked, pointing at the smoking foil pack still on the fire.

"Er—yeah, I had planned on it."

"Well, you'd better get it off the fire then," she replied, disappointed, sitting back on the bench.

"Sorry, I don't bring that much out with me." She wasn't about to mention that Cat had just eaten tomorrow's dinner. "There's some granola in the pack, though."

Cat brightened. "Great!" She dove into the pack and came out with the big bag of granola, and began to funnel it into her mouth.

"Weren't you planning on camping out here this weekend? Where's all your stuff?"

"I forgot."

"You forgot to bring *anything* with you?"

Cat set down the bag, now mostly empty. "Yup. Lucky for me you're out here, right?"

"Sure." Andie took a bite of her slightly charred food and let the warmth radiate through her chest. Damn, it really was getting cold in these woods this time of year. "So what do you do?"

"Do you always interrogate strangers?"

"You know what *my* job is."

Cat shrugged. "Bit of this, bit of that. Not everyone's life is centered on a career, you know."

"Well, no, but—"

"Asking people about their jobs is a quick way to make them feel shitty about where they're at in life."

"Sorry," Andie apologized again, aware it was her fourth apology since meeting Cat. This really wasn't going well at all. "Hobbies?" she tried.

"I am an amateur horticulturist!" Cat replied enthusiastically.

"Oh, plants."

"What do you mean, 'oh, plants?' Plants represent the basic building blocks of life, they're so incredibly diverse and fascinating, and—and that's why I'm out here this weekend, actually. I'm researching some threatened species, like the yellow dogtooth violet, also known as the trout lily, which is probably more apt since it's not actually a violet, I'm hoping to find some to relocate to safer areas where they won't be stepped on by the half-ripe avocado dense-heads we have running around these woods."

"I can't imagine the park rangers would be thrilled with you digging up threatened plants—" Andie started. "Oh, that's why you don't like them."

"Among other reasons, but yes. Other parks have whole conservation teams, but after funding cuts this reserve is stuck with some up-jumped rent-a-cops that don't do much other than evict people living in the backwoods in tents, or people like you, camping outside the allowed pitches."

"Funding cuts is a good reason to be invested in politics."

Cat raised an eyebrow. "Yeah, okay, I'll allow that point." She looked up and the moon and visibly shivered. "Getting cold. Didn't think I'd be out this long."

"I thought you were planning on camping all weekend?"

"Something like that. Throw another log on the fire, will you?"

Andie tossed a big one into the fire, sending sparks into the air. "How's that?"

"Yeah. Good." Cat reached out her slender fingers to warm them, scooting closer to the fire. "It's getting late, are you planning on sleeping at some point?"

"I only have a one-person tent..."

"Don't worry about that. I'm kind of a night owl. I'll stick with the fire if you want to turn in."

"Hm..." Andie hesitated. The forest might be full of wood, but not all of it was suitable for burning, and she didn't want this stranger to burn through all her firewood. "Can you make sure you leave me some logs for tomorrow night?"

"Sure. You sticking around, then? Even with the imaginary bear?"

"I have to look for my camera. It must be near that clearing where I saw the *very real and terrifying* bear."

"Alright, well, see you in the morning. Sleep tight. Don't let the bears bite," Cat said with an exaggerated wink.

"Heh. Night."

* * *

"Hey! You! You can't be here!"

Andie's eyes flew open, and she sat up in the tent, soggy from the waist down. Turns out the rain had come, after all. If she could still find her camera, water damage was costly to repair. Her heart sank in her chest.

"Did you hear me? Come out of there, right now!"

"Alright, alright! Give me a second!" she shouted back, struggling to disentangle herself from her wet sleeping bag. She shivered, despite the morning sun. Unzipping the tent flap, she stuck her head outside and squinted in the light. A park ranger was standing at her extinguished campfire, clipboard in hand.

"You're not authorized to be camping in this area, young lady." Andie snorted. At thirty-four years old, it wasn't exactly accurate. "Is something funny?" the ranger demanded. "Because all I'm seeing here is a gross negligence and disrespect for the rules of this reserve. Who knows what fragile ecosystems you might have disturbed? And a campfire? Frankly, it's an outrage!"

"The campfire was within a ring, and it was tended and put out," Andie argued. "But fine, whatever, I'll pack up. I wasn't planning on staying another night, anyway."

"I'll be escorting you to the park gates immediately, in fact."

"What? No! My tent, and my gear—"

"Will all be made available to you at lost and found in due time, which you can collect once your ban has expired."

Andie climbed clumsily out of the tent, her sock catching on the zippered closure. "Hang on, what do you mean *ban*?"

The ranger smirked, her long, red braid like flames in the early light. "You will be banned from this reserve for three weeks."

"That's not fair!" She'd never get a good shot, now. Her dreams of winning the wildlife competition were exploding into smoke.

"Come with me, I will take you to the gates, where I assume your vehicle is illegally parked?"

"Can you just give me a minute?" Andie shouted. "I just need to take a five minute walk in that direction, where I dropped my camera last night—"

"Do I look stupid to you? You'll just take off into the woods and leave before I confirm your car registration."

"You can even come with me if you want, but my camera, please—"

"If anyone turns in a camera, you will be able to collect it from the information desk along with the rest of your things in three weeks."

Andie stuffed her wet feet into her boots. "Listen, lady, my camera is my livelihood. I just need *five* minutes."

"Well, maybe you should have thought about that before breaking the rules of Pine Meadows Reserve! I am duty bound to keep this park safe from transients and poachers, and—"

"What am I going to poach with a camera, a photo?"

"And that's another thing - any pictures taken in the reserve must be credited to us and approved by the director."

"You realize this is fucking absurd, right?" Andie shot back, picking up her camera bag. No camera, but at least she still had her extra lenses and tripod. "If the director really cared about the safety and preservation of this forest, they'd clamp down on the assholes driving in from out of state for photo opportunities and leaving their crap everywhere!"

"Tourism is what keeps this park open, I'll have you know. Now come on, it's time to go."

It was time to change tactics, if she was going to get her camera back. "Ranger..." she trailed off, looking for the badge. "Ranger Dade? I understand the pressures you are under, especially in the light of last year's budget cuts, but if you could just spare a few minutes for me to find my camera—"

"Absolutely not."

"You don't have to be such a hard ass, you know. It wouldn't cost you anything to just give me a minute to find my camera!"

"Maybe next time you won't go trespassing and getting yourself into trouble. Parts of the reserve are closed to the public for a reason, you know." Ranger Dade tapped on her clipboard. "You didn't see anything unusual, did you?"

Andie swallowed hard. Something told her not to tell the ranger about the bear. "Unusual, like what?"

"Poachers, unauthorized rock climbers." She paused. "Invasive species."

"If I said yes, would you let me find my camera?"

"No."

"Then no, I didn't see anything unusual."

The ranger's face clouded with anger. "Enough of this crap, I'm taking you to your vehicle and banning you for three weeks."

"But—"

"Any more delays, and I'll make it four."

Andie clenched her jaw. "Fine," she said, through gritted teeth.

CHAPTER TWO

Cat shifted her beat up old truck into park and shoved the keys into her jeans pocket. She yawned and checked her phone, scrolling through the apps that paid her rent. If she was quick, she might be able to grab a quick nap before heading out to do some rideshares later, maybe some food delivery if she wasn't too tired. Shifts always took it out of her.

Slamming the door shut behind her, she had to jam the lock to keep it from drifting open again. Shitty landlord wouldn't fix it, but what else was new? That asshole owned half the goddamn town, and now part of the reserve, too.

"Hey Sis," her sister Anita mumbled, sliding into one of the kitchen chairs. "You look like shit. Bad shift?"

"The worst. You wouldn't believe how many people are out lately." Anita poured herself a bowl of cereal, spilling bits on the ground with a gentle cardboard tinkle. "Where the hell did you run off to last night, anyway?"

"Research. And trying to keep tabs on some of the newbies up at the reserve."

"That ranger still giving you a hard time?"

"I'm still managing to keep two steps ahead of her, at least. For now, anyway." Cat sat in the other chair and grabbed the box of cereal, pouring some directly into her mouth. "Where's everyone else?"

Anita shrugged. "I never know what they get up to when their shifts are done."

"As long as they don't wind up dead in a ditch somewhere. You know how things are these days. You can never be too careful."

"Yeah, yeah. You don't have to lecture me all the time, you know."

"Any word from Mom and Dad?"

"Is there ever?"

Cat crunched on her cereal. "True." Their parents had never quite forgiven them for leaving the Pacific Northwest in search of greener pastures and better jobs. Worse still was that those things hadn't even appeared yet, despite constant searching. "Any plans today?"

"Sleep. Class later, then I have a shift tonight."

"Need me to drive you?"

"Nah."

"So how's school?"

Anita rolled her eyes. "Honestly, Catriona, can you ever just let me eat in peace? Not everyone can be so bright and bushy-tailed after a night shift."

"Hm." Cat scowled at the use of her full name. She let the sound of Anita's spoon scraping against the bottom of the bowl be the only noise for a moment before continuing. "You know I love you, right?"

"Caaaaaat," her sister protested, pouring another bowl of cereal. "I know. And I love you, but you really need to find someone else to bother in the mornings."

"Okay, okay, I hear you. I just feel like we never really talk anymore."

"We're talking right now!"

"You're *yelling* at me right now, I'd hardly call that talking," Cat grumbled.

"Fine, what are we having for dinner?"

"Whatever you can find in the freezer."

Anita poked at her cereal with her water-stained spoon. "There's nothing good in there. We're all out of those frozen burrito things."

"I know," Cat said with a sigh. "But I'm flat broke until the next pay cycle, I had to throw some money at the city so they wouldn't turn off the water."

"If you finished your nursing degree..."

"You know that's impossible with the night shifts. I tried."

"I just feel like maybe if you time it right—"

"It's not gonna happen, Anita. It just doesn't work, not right now." Cat pushed the box of cereal away. "Maybe not ever."

"You said that I should finish my program—"

"That's different, you're a graphic designer. You can work whenever you want, once you have a decent client list. And with your people skills, I bet you're raking it in six months after that diploma is in your hands."

"We'll see about that," Anita muttered, before draining her bowl and wiping her mouth with the back of her pale, freckled hand. "I still think you should think about trying again, Cat. You're so good at it, and we could move out, get our own place—"

The door crashed open, and two barely college-aged boys staggered in.

"Cat! We missed you last night!"

"Morning, Luke. I had to leave early, I had some stuff to do."

"Stuff like what? It's not like you to knock off a shift early."

"*Stuff.*"

"Hey Felix, you think it has anything to do with that hot woman wandering around the reserve that she was complaining about?"

"I think it might," Felix said, an irritating grin spreading across his face. "Did you meet someone nice, Cat?"

"Go away, you both smell like roadkill."

"Aww, don't be like that! You know we love you, Mama bear!"

Cat grimaced. "I told you goons not to call me that, I'm barely ten years older than you."

"Yeah, but you let us follow you when you two left the west coast," Luke said, more seriously this time. "Me and Felix would probably still be running around in the streets if you hadn't let us tag along."

"You barely gave me a choice," Cat said with a smirk.

"We know, we know," Felix said, hugging her shoulders from behind. "Just know, we are grateful for giving us a place." He tilted his head at Anita. "And you, too, for putting up with our bullshit."

Anita smirked. "Yeah, and there's plenty of it, coming from you two." She wrinkled her nose and made a retching noise. "God, Cat was right, you *do* smell like roadkill. What the hell were you doing on your shift, scraping it off the highway?"

"Ah, Nita, you know we have better taste than that," Luke said, ruffling her hair.

"Fuck off!" she shouted with a laugh, waving him away. "I have shit to do."

"Okay, bye!" Felix shouted, bounding out of the kitchen, dragging Luke with him. Their noise could be heard through the walls, the slamming of dresser drawers, the squabble about who would shower first, the heavy clambering on the bare wood flooring of the hallway.

"Who even knows what they got up to last night," Anita said, picking a piece of fluff off her pajamas.

"Whoa, wait just a minute. I know why *I* don't know what they were doing, but why don't you?"

"I dunno, Cat, maybe I just wanted to work by myself last night."

"Anita!"

"Don't get all upset, I was careful!"

"What if someone had seen you?" Cat bit her tongue, knowing her own hypocrisy. The cute woman by the campfire had been too much to ignore.

Anita scraped the legs of the chair back and picked up the cereal bowl from the table. "No one saw me."

"But what if they had?"

"Stop worrying about stuff that didn't happen!"

"Of course I worry! You're my sister!"

"I might be your sister, but I'm also a grown woman, I'm older than the boys, and you let them do shifts alone."

Cat brushed off the knees of her jeans. "That's different because they aren't alone, they go together."

"Not always."

"Well, I'll talk to them about that, obviously. I just don't think it's a good idea. It's dangerous. There are so many people moving through town now, we don't know where most of them are from, they don't live around here, can't trust them."

"*You* go out alone."

"That's different because... because it just is."

"It's a good thing you don't have kids, Cat, because that excuse sucks."

Cat laughed. "Alright, I hear you, just... be careful. Please. I don't know what I'd do if any of you went missing."

"We're not going to go missing. Stop worrying all the time. Go to sleep, Sis, don't you have work later?"

"Yeah."

"Then what are you still doing in here? Go!"

"Where's today's paper?"

Anita washed her bowl and set it in the dish rack. "What do you need that for?" she asked, her tone a little too even to be believable.

"Why, what's wrong?"

Her sister sighed. "I didn't want to tell you til later. I wanted you to get some rest."

"Well, I'm definitely not going to get any making up worst-case scenarios while I stare at the back of my eyelids. Come on, out with it."

"Here." Anita slapped the day's newspaper on the paper. "The zoning board is allowing the reserve development to move forward."

"What? No!"

"Yeah. And it gets worse - the company buying it wants to turn it into luxury condos."

Cat barked out a laugh. "For who? I don't see many high rollers around here!" She thumbed through the newspaper, swallowing back a growl when she found her answer. "You can't be serious that it's going to be owned and operated by Syndicorp."

"They said they'd be creating jobs here, that's why it passed the board."

"That's bullshit."

"Yeah, we know it's bullshit, but if the board voted it down, people would claim they're trying to keep the town from growing."

"It doesn't need to grow! It's fine as it is, without people coming in here and jacking up the rents, bulldozing half the goddamn forest..."

Anita leaned against the peeling kitchen counter. "We could always move."

"With what money?"

"We'll figure it out."

"I'm tired of moving, Nita. What's it been, six times in four years?"

"What other options are there? I mean, we can wait it out as long as we can, but you know as soon as they break ground this place is going to be swarming."

Cat sighed heavily, smoothing the paper out on the table. "We could try to round up some protest signatures to deliver to the board?"

"Do you really think that will work?"

"No. But it might buy us some time while we figure out what to do."

"People won't be happy, they'll see you as trying to keep them from better jobs. They're not going to believe that the company will reduce that down. People never do."

"Well, I've got to figure out something, or we'll be running forever. From higher rents, from..."

Anita turned toward the window to hide the tears gathering at the corners of her eyes. "Sometimes it makes me wish we'd never left the coast."

"It was the right thing to do."

"Yeah. But it was nice to have a place we knew we belonged."

"As long as we didn't question anything."

"Heh. Remember that time Mom found out that we were thinking about going to college?"

"She hit the roof." Cat snorted. "Literally."

"I'm sorry, I know this is hard for you, too. I'm probably just tired."

"Go to bed, then. You want company on your shift tonight?"

Cat smiled. "Yeah, that would be nice."

* * *

"Alright, thanks, leave me a review!" Cat shouted as the business man climbed out of the backseat of her four-door truck. Folks dressed like that never left her a positive review. They always complained about the rust on her truck and the small tears in the fabric upholstery. As far as she was concerned, why care about what a vehicle looks like, if it's just to get you from point A to point B? These assholes never tipped, either.

The man didn't reply. He marched straight up to the doors of the three-story building without a word.

"I bet he's one of those Syndicorp assholes," Anita said.

"Probably."

"I hope his whites in the laundry always turn out slightly pink."

Cat laughed. "Me, too." She tapped through the apps, ignoring the rippled itch that cascaded across her skin. "Alright, who's next?"

"Looks like a food delivery from the pizza place to one of those big houses near the reserve."

"No, I don't want that one. Those houses never tip, and they're rude."

"Alright, well… how about a ride from the square out towards the edge of town?"

"Yeah, we'll take that." Cat switched on her turn signal and pulled onto the empty road. "You heard from the boys?"

"No."

"They better not be doing shifts alone."

"I think they planned to head up to the river, so they're probably going together."

"Good." The street lights were starting to come on, and the sun would set soon. The itch intensified, but Cat resisted scratching. That never helped, anyway.

Anita tugged at her seatbelt. "What do you think will happen once half the reserve is gone?"

"Budget cuts. They'll keep promoting the rest of the reserve to picture hunters to keep revenue up." She sighed. "We'll have to find another place."

"The next nearest reserve is hours away. Well, the next one largest, anyway. There are some smaller ones, but they're crammed full with barbecue grills and playgrounds."

"I know. But if we move before you graduate, before the boys finish their apprenticeships… then everything we've worked so hard to build will be gone. We'll have to start over."

"We've started over before."

"I'm sick of it. At least before we were close enough to keep commuting to school, but if we're hours away, well, it's a whole mess, isn't it?"

"The boys would understand."

"I hate that people like us struggle so much. It makes it so that the only ones who succeed, or have stability, are the ones who stay in places like we lived in the northwest. I just want to build something different, but it's impossible to even get started. The world just isn't built for us."

Her sister leaned her head on Cat's shoulder. "If anyone can build it, it's you. You're a force of nature."

"Thanks." Cat smiled, and turned on the headlights as she pulled up to the curb. "Alright, where the hell is this chick? I can't park here, I'll get a ticket."

"I don't see anyone."

"God dammit, these people, I—Hi! Are you Sharon?"

"Yeah, I'm Sharon."

"Hi Sharon, you can just sit yourself in the back and we'll get going to your destination."

"This truck looks like a piece of shit. They let you rideshare with this deathtrap?"

Cat bristled. "It runs just fine."

"The new app everyone is using requires the cars to look nice."

"Then maybe you should use the new app," Cat said through gritted teeth, smiling at Sharon in the rear-view mirror. "Won't be long," she continued, pulling the truck off the main street and onto the residential street that ran to the end of town. Three miles of sparse houses, some with long driveways and huge, ten-foot wrought-iron gates locked with a key pad. Some of them sat empty most of the time, used as accommodation for people looking for a party house, or a cute aesthetic place to take photos before they headed back to their overpriced highrise apartments in the city, with their perfectly curated homes and empty bookshelves.

"What is there to do for fun in this place?" Sharon asked. "I'm here on business."

Ah, Cat thought, another Syndicorp employee. They were multiplying like rabbits. "Well, there's the bar in town, but it looks like you just came from there."

"Is that it?"

Anita snorted.

"Uh, well, I think the grocery store in the next county is twenty-four hours."

Cat didn't want to mention the reserve, and this woman probably already knew about it anyway, if she was here on Syndicorp business. "There's a bowling alley uptown, but it's only open until nine."

"*Bowling*," Sharon scoffed, tapping a note into her phone. "That just won't do. Are you sure there's nothing else?"

"Er, no, not really. I think the buffet is open until eleven on the weekends."

"Then what do you people do here for nightlife?"

"All due respect, but most people work too much and have too little to be going to nightclubs, but there's one about an hour east if you want to drive. It's called Thorns."

"What's it like on the inside?"

Cat pulled the steering wheel to the left for the turn. "Dark."

"It's no wonder you only have a two-star rating with this attitude," Sharon said, tapping angrily into her phone.

"I don't go to nightclubs much."

"Well, you should, maybe it would dislodge that Podunk stick that's up your ass. Maybe you'd meet a nice man who would offer to get rid of it for you."

Anita began to shake with silent laughter.

"I'm alright, thanks," Cat retorted, pulling into the driveway of one of the huge, mass produced mansions with the ugly, mismatched edifices. "We're here." She turned in her seat and grinned at Sharon. "Thanks for riding with us today! Please leave us a five-star review and request us the next time you need to travel in Applefield!" The saccharine sweet tone even irritated herself, and when she turned back to face forward, she wrinkled her nose.

"Whatever," Sharon said, climbing out of the truck and slamming the door a little too hard.

Cat's phone chimed sadly. A one-star review. Typical.

"Oh my God," Anita said between fits of giggles. "What an absolute asshole. Maybe you'd meet a nice *man*, Sis."

"Gross."

"Are you ready to go to the reserve yet? I'm getting antsy."

"I have one more stop I have to make."

CHAPTER THREE

"Good morning, Daisy," Andie said to her chinchilla, which was sleeping peacefully in its large cage that took up most of the open space in her small studio apartment. She never could live totally alone, even if she was without human companionship. Sometimes, Daisy was enough.

She was still mourning the loss of her camera. She'd called the reserve information office twice a day for two days, hoping for news someone had turned it in, but there was nothing. If someone did find it now, the damage would be extensive. The contract work had been lost as a result, and now she was staring down a negative bank balance. *Fucking hell*, she thought. *Could things get any worse?*

The fridge was empty, and the pantry was pretty much bare. It would be cheap instant noodles for breakfast, again. She'd have to figure out something, and fast, if she was going to pay her rent on time. The landlord was especially fond of charging a ninety dollar late fee, which was another thing she really couldn't afford. Maybe she could pick up some gig work to make up the difference. For now, though, she was about to be running late for her job photographing empty properties for the local real estate developer - at least they had their own equipment she could use, if she needed to. Rumor had it they were working on a big deal to build a big block of new buildings near the reserve, and if it went ahead, it would mean a nice chunk of money for Andie.

That was months away, though, and she was broke as hell right *now*.

"I have to go, Daisy," she announced to her sleeping pet. "I'll be back after work. I promise I won't be late." She set fresh hay into the cage gently, so as not to disturb her, and gave her some clean water, too. "Maybe later I'll give you some treats, if you're good." Daisy continued to sleep.

Andie eased open the door and locked it behind her, before almost tripping over a box on her welcome mat, the flickering light from the failing fluorescent bulbs in the ceiling flashing across the unsealed flaps. There was no address or return label, and it was sitting open. Was it something one of the neighbor kids left? She picked up the box, the cardboard smooth in her hands. Lifting one of the flaps, she gasped. It was her camera.

Looking up and down the hallway, whoever had left it was long gone - but it was definitely her camera. She flicked the switch, willing it to power on, almost praying that it wasn't irreparably damaged. To her relief, the screen came alive, framing the floor of her apartment building in little green squares. "Yes!" Andie squealed with excitement. She turned the camera over in her hands, looking for any visible damage, and found none. Strange, considering she knew it had rained the night she lost it.

The information desk must have delivered it, who else would know that it was hers? Even stranger that they hadn't mentioned it when she had called just an hour ago, right after she dragged herself out of bed. It must have been delivered the night before, because there was nothing on her mat when she got home for dinner. She'd been home the whole time, though, and it was odd that no one had at least knocked to let her know it was there. Andie was glad to have it back, but still irritated that someone had left such an expensive piece of equipment outside her door without saying anything.

Tucking the camera back in its box, and the box under her arm, she speed-walked to the door and out to her old, reliable blue two-door hatchback. It was old enough to drink, if it was human, and sometimes it felt like it was, like last winter when she was pleading with it to get them home safe. It had, despite the nearly bald tires on the back wheels. She set the box on the passenger's seat and fired it into gear, setting off for today's photography location two towns away, where there was a renovated building ready to go up for sale. The apartment stager, the person who filled it with rented furniture to make it look more appealing in photos, had finished the day before.

The roads were quiet, which Andie was grateful for. There weren't many traffic jams in Applefield, but she couldn't afford to be any later than she already was. She couldn't lose this job, too, even if it was almost criminally underpaid. She was making excellent time, even at the speed limit, so much so that she made up for waking up twenty minutes late, and she pulled into the parking lot of a coffee shop she knew that was excellent. Bells on the door tinkled as she pushed it open, greeted with the warm aroma of hot coffee and freshly baked cinnamon buns. Her stomach growled loudly.

"Hey, Andie!" the woman behind the counter shouted, her long dark hair tied up in a ponytail. "It's nice to see you round here again."

"Hi, Mara." Andie dug through the bottom of her beaten-up messenger bag, hunting for some spare change. Her bank card sure as hell wasn't going to work, but the quarters might buy her a tiny bit of happiness, while they definitely wouldn't pay any of the bills she had lined up. "What's good today?"

"Everything you like," Mara joked. "Thanks again for those promo photos for our social media, everyone is raving about them, and business is up on last month."

"That's great!"

"You really should have let us pay you for them."

Andie waved her away. "Don't be silly. I want to help local places, especially ones that have such delicious coffee." She was only able to come up with two dollars and forty-five cents from the bottom of her bag, all in loose change. "Uh, just a drip coffee for me today. Black."

Mara looked at her with concern. "I'll get you your favorite. And don't worry, it's on the house."

"No!" Andie protested. "You guys are working so hard, and—"

"Andie. Stop. You help us, we help you." Mara selected a fat, juicy cinnamon roll from the case with a pair of long tons, and put it into the toaster oven to warm up. "You really should come around more, liven the place up during the midday slump."

"Nah, I'd cramp your style."

"You're always welcome here, you know." Mara tapped the filter on the counter and slid it into the machine. "Even if your snotty friends prefer to get coffee at the chain up the street."

"Heh." Andie hadn't heard from them in nearly two weeks. It made her feel alone. "They just don't want to get addicted to how good the coffee is here."

"Make sure you drag their asses in here sometime, okay? We need them to bring the rest of their snotty friends in, because that's where all the money is."

"Next time I hear from them," Andie promised. Whenever that would be.

"Here you go," Mara said, handing her a brown paper bag with the hot cinnamon roll and a paper cup with a plastic lid. "One white chocolate raspberry latte, extra whip."

"Thank you, this means a lot, really—"

"It's nothing. Are you sure you can't stop in later?"

Andie shook her head. "I'll be working until five at least."

The door bells chimed again, and Andie instinctively moved away from the counter to make room for the paying customers. She crinkled the top of the bag and held the coffee in her hands, relishing the warmth on such a frigid morning.

"Honestly, Luke, you're such a pain in the ass sometimes," a woman said with a laugh. A familiar voice, and an even more familiar laugh. Andie blinked. It was the woman from the reserve, dressed in a grey sweater dress and knee-high boots, cute little silver hoops hugging her earlobes. She looked even better than she had in the woods, covered in mud and a torn up old jacket.

"Hey," Andie said, her voice squeakier than she would have liked. "It's Cat, right?" She knew her name was Cat, obviously, but was trying hard to seem cooler than she was.

Cat turned and flinched. "Oh. It's you."

"It was... nice meeting you. The other night. In the reserve." Cat just stared, and embarrassment began to creep up Andie's spine. Why did she always have to be so awkward? "Anyway, I'd better be going—"

"Wait." Cat shook her head. "I'm sorry, you just took me by surprise."

"Do I look that hideous in the light of day?"

"No, no, it's just—"

"You look nice." As soon as she said it, Andie swallowed back a nervous cough. She was always a mess around pretty girls, and her first interaction

25

with Cat had proved it. "I just mean, you look different. In a dress. And, you know, makeup and stuff."

Cat furrowed her brow. "Well I'm hardly going to wear my best when I'm traipsing around the forest, am I?"

"Whoa, whoa, whoa," Luke interrupted. "You met her during your shift? Isn't that what you're always telling *us* not to do?"

"Shut up," Cat said through gritted teeth. "We'll talk about it later."

"Just wait until I tell Anita—"

"I said shut up! Now I'm leaving, enjoy your shift."

"I thought you said you wanted—"

"Luke!" Cat hissed.

"Alright, alright," he said, grabbing an apron from the hook by the register and hanging it over his head. "Pick me up at seven, please, Mama Bear."

Cat closed her eyes. "I said not to call me that!"

Andie looked from one of them to the other. "You don't look old enough to be his mom, unless you've found the fountain of youth."

"I'm not, he's just a numbskull." Cat fidgeted with the small purple card wallet in her hands. "Sorry, he's just—"

"It's fine, really."

"Anyway, I—"

"I didn't realize you worked at the reserve," Andie interrupted. "Sorry. You first."

"No, I don't, it's—uh, it's complicated. I do research out there. Plants. And stuff."

The coffee in Andie's hand started to burn her palm. "Right, I remember. Amateur horticulturist." She squinted, and then the pieces started to come together. "Hang on, it was you who found my camera, it has to be! There was no water damage, and there was that rainstorm that night—I don't know where you went, but—"

"Shh!" Cat pulled her by the elbow to the far side of the cafe just as another group walked in. "Yes, it was me, but I probably shouldn't have, there are strict rules, and I could get into a lot of trouble."

"For talking to me?" Andie shook her head. "I don't know who you work for, but don't worry, I won't say anything."

"You should really stay out of that part of the reserve. It's dangerous."

Andie searched her face for an answer. "Why?"

"Poachers."

"What would they be poaching in there?"

"Deer, mostly. The rangers don't do anything about it, and you could wind up shot if you're not careful."

"Is that... a threat?"

"No! I'm just saying, there are some dangerous people in there, and they'll shoot anything that moves. They don't know other people are back there."

Andie shrugged. "I'll wear orange, then."

"They don't want to be seen on camera. They'll destroy evidence of their poaching." Cat squeezed her elbow gently, and it sent a jolt through Andie's body. "Do you understand?"

"Uh, yeah. Sure."

"Take care, Andie."

"Wait - how did you find my address?"

Cat tilted her head, and a smile played at the edges of her mouth. "You're not hard to find online."

"Maybe you could find me again sometime?" As soon as the words were out of Andie's mouth, she wished she could take them back. Stupid, awkward Andie. "Uh, I mean—you know what? Never mind. I have to go, actually, I'm late for work." She turned and strode for the door, each step widening as she aimed to escape the awkward encounter she'd created for herself.

"Andie, wait—"

She got into her car and drove five miles above the speed limit, all the way to the work location, desperate to get as far away as she could. *Damn,* she thought, pulling into a parking space. *Forgot my storage card.* The development agency office had a spare camera, but she had to bring her own card. She pulled her own camera from the box, and flipped open the slot. The SD card, and all the photos she'd taken at the reserve, were gone.

* * *

Andie flopped onto her old but comfortable bed and wrapped herself up in the hand-knitted blanket her grandmother had given her before she died. It was just as important as her camera to her, but irreplaceable. It was the one thing she would save, if forced to choose.

Her dinner was a microwaveable platter of bland chicken and watery pasta, not particularly tasty, but it was cheap, and she'd rescued it from the back of the small freezer. Whatever she could do to stretch food out until she got paid from the development company again, the better. She'd emailed the canceled work, saying that she could do it now that she had her camera back, but they'd already hired someone else. It's not like there was a shortage of product photographers looking for work, especially as full-time photography jobs were going the way of the dinosaurs. Everything was freelance and contract work, nowadays.

"Is that tasty, Daisy?" Andie asked the chinchilla, who was happily munching away on some fresh salad greens. "I got them special for you, I know how you like that kind." Daisy continued to crunch on the lettuce, the quiet sounds Andie's only company.

She checked her phone again. No messages. She texted her friends again: "*Did you change your numbers?*" Her previous message had been left on read. Was she being ghosted? Did it even matter, anymore? There was nothing on television, just re-runs of old shows she'd seen a hundred times. Another boring night alone.

Her camera was sitting on top of the cheap plywood kitchen table, miraculously undamaged. She was so grateful that Cat had rescued it for her, but the missing SD card still bothered her. How would it have fallen out of the latched slot? If Cat had taken it, *why?* The only photos on there would be from that night in the reserve, some blurry images of the bear, if she was lucky, but nothing else. She always took a clean card to work on wildlife photography. When you were shooting in RAW, it took up a lot of digital space.

Andie did a couple of searches on her phone for women named Cat in the area. She figured she must work for some local conservation groups or something, but she couldn't find any trace of a group like that. Frustrated, she tossed her phone to the other side of the couch. Her investigative skills had never been that good, and Cat was impossible to find. She definitely hadn't grown up here - there was only one high school, a small one, and Andie definitely would have remembered a girl as pretty as her. As it was, Andie didn't date at all in school, and didn't kiss a girl until she went away to college. What a mess that had been.

She paced back and forth from the stove to the bed, only a few steps between them, but in a small studio apartment, there wasn't much option. Daisy watched her with curiosity. Andie was antsy, like she wanted to do something, but wasn't sure what. It was more than boredom, but not quite impulsiveness. If the SD card *had* fallen out, it might still be at the reserve. She'd already purchased a new one, she had for work that morning, but something about it was nagging at her.

The calendar hanging on the wall marked off the days until the competition deadline. It was only a couple of weeks away, now. She was banned from the park until the new year, thanks to her arguing with the ranger on the long hike back to the information building. What an absolute piece of work. What kind of person wouldn't let you at least look for your camera, or pack up your gear? Now all her stuff was held hostage in the building until her ban was over, which meant driving further to camp in a different reserve wasn't going to be an option, either.

Andie continued to pace, the thick strands of her cozy socks catching on the uneven floorboards. She picked up her phone. No messages. She tried another search, this time for women named Catherine. What else could "Cat" be short for? She wanted to ask about the SD card. She wanted to apologize for running out that morning. She was strangely drawn to her, and not just because she was the cutest, prettiest woman she'd ever met. Maybe her name was spelled with a K. She searched for Katherine, and then Katia. The only result on the last one was an eighty-seven-year-old woman who lived in one of the mansions at the edge of town.

"Screw it," she said aloud. "I'm not afraid of a goddamn ranger." Securing the camera around her neck, she swapped in a fresh SD card and swung the tripod over her back by its strap. She grabbed her keys from the hook at the door, shoved her feet into her boots, so caked with mud that they left reverse imprints with dirt on the floor, and headed out the door. She was going to go back to the reserve, and she'd either find her SD card, or she'd find Cat, or she'd find the bear.

CHAPTER FOUR

Cat pulled into the reserve, wearing the gross night shift clothes again. She hated wearing torn up old plaid and dirty jeans, but there was no sense in wearing something cute, not when it would just get ruined.

The parking lot was rammed full, which would have been strange, once, especially on a weeknight. Not anymore, though - the garbage cans were already overflowing, and trash was spread all over the ground. Cat grimaced at the mess and stepped over a discarded styrofoam cup. *Pigs*, she thought.

She slung her backpack over her shoulder and headed for the red trail, the one that led the furthest away from the main encampment. Once the housing development started bulldozing the back half of the reserve, things would get a lot more difficult. The thought of it made bile rise up in the back of her throat, and her stomach roil angrily. Why couldn't people just leave wild areas the hell alone, instead of developing them, sanitizing them with perfectly trimmed lawns and sculpted, limited gardens with smooth paved stones that encouraged you to walk the way they had intended you to? It was sick.

"Excuse me!" a ranger said, running at her full speed. "You need to sign in!"

"What? Since when?"

"I've seen you in here at the same time the past five nights, we have reason to believe you might be a poacher."

Cat barked out a laugh. "Lady, you couldn't be further from the truth. Besides, what makes you think the poachers are coming in through the front goddamn gate? They're obviously jumping the fences at the far end of the reserve."

"How would you know that, if you're not a poacher?"

"Are you serious right now?"

The ranger held up a clipboard. "Sign in, or you're not going any further."

"I'm not signing in, this is *public land*." She gestured around. "Did you ask any of these little piggies to sign in?"

"Yes, of course, and the only person to give me grief on it is the one person I've suspected might be connected to illegal activities in the park."

Cat turned and walked towards the trail head. "Sign in for me, then. Name's Ruby Delacroix."

"Excuse me, no," the ranger said, speed-walking to catch up to her. "You have to show an ID."

"Is there a law against hiking, now?"

"What kind of normal person hikes in the dark? Answer me that!"

"One who doesn't like people."

The ranger side stepped her and stood in front of the trail head sign, blocking her path. "ID, or I'm calling the police."

"For hiking?"

"For refusing to comply, and suspicion of connection with illegal poaching activities."

Cat really didn't have time to deal with rent-a-cops, much less real ones. "Fine." She pulled her license from the wallet in her pocket and flashed it. "Catriona Evans. Sign me in."

"That's not the same name you said a minute ago."

"No, I just wanted you to leave me alone."

"I'm afraid you'll have to come with me," the ranger said, hand on her radio, "to confirm this ID is genuine."

"You people are completely off the mark, you know that, right?" Her skin itched, but there was no point in scratching.

"It won't take long."

Cat followed the ranger back to the information building. This is what she got for going in through the front gate. She'd sneak in where the poachers did, if she wasn't afraid she'd get shot for it. The yellowed fluorescent lights buzzed, and the silhouette of a dead fly flickered. Budget cuts, indeed. She thrust her ID at the ranger. "Here."

"Take a seat, please."

"I thought you said this wouldn't take long."

"It won't. Fifteen, twenty minutes maybe."

The sun had set already, and Cat was growing restless. The ranger was moving in slow motion, and Cat knew she couldn't hold it in much longer. She shifted in her chair. "What if I just head out, and I'll come back for my ID?"

"That's silly. What if the ID was fake? You wouldn't come back for it."

"It's not fake."

"That's what someone with a fake ID would say." The ranger dialed a number on the old rotary phone. Why the hell did they still even have that in here? The molasses level slowness was worse than a medieval torture device. "Hello, I need to check an ID for veracity. Yes, it's Catriona Evans." The ranger turned and faced the wall. "No, that's Catriona with a C." She wound the cord around her finger. "No, it's C as in cat, A as in... antelope, T as in... T-Rex..." she trailed off. "No, T-Rex like the dinosaur. Yes, like the movie! I loved it, saw it in theaters twice. Didn't care for the man, though. No, I hadn't heard there was a sequel!"

Cat groaned audibly. If this took much longer, she'd never finish her shift before sunrise. If it took much longer, she'd have a lot more questions to answer than just her name.

"Evans, you know, like it sounds. Yeah." The ranger turned back to face her. "Petite, short, dark hair. No, she's not wearing glasses - oh hang on, someone is trying to get through on the radio. I'll call you right back."

"For fuck's sake!" Cat growled. "Obviously it's not fake, can I go now?"

"Not until I confirm with the registry office," the ranger said, grabbing at her radio. "Go for Dade."

"We've got civilian reports on the back nine that a female is scaling the fence. Five foot ten or so, dark braid, camera bag."

Andie, you adorable fucking fool, Cat thought, squirming in her chair. She couldn't just let it go, stay safe at home, no, she had to come back, and not even through the gap in the fence. Amateur.

"On it, Officer," the ranger replied, grabbing an extra set of handcuffs from the desk. "I'll head out that way right now." Clipping the radio back on her belt, she turned to Cat. "You, stay here until I get back, and we'll get this ID problem sorted. Don't go anywhere. If you do, you'll be de facto banned permanently."

Cat ground her teeth, the muscles in her thighs cramping. "You got it."

The ranger got into an all-terrain-vehicle and sped off into the woods, swerving around the No Civilian Vehicles sign. Cat jumped off the chair as soon as the ranger was out of site and snatched her license and the paperwork from the clipboard. With any luck, the ranger wouldn't remember her name. She couldn't wait around any longer, she had a shift to do, and besides, her sister was waiting for her already on the east end of the park.

The information building door slammed behind her, and Cat tore off for the trail head, ignoring the shouts from the partiers in the nearby pitches. She didn't care if they ratted her out to the ranger, she'd have much bigger problems if she stayed. Missing a shift was the worst thing she could do. The moon started to crest over the distant horizon, the tops of the trees still invisible in the darkness. The cold wind blew through her hair, and she felt *alive*. This is what the forest was supposed to be, wild and dangerous, not curated and manicured.

She paused at the trail fork, her feet sinking in the wet soil. The right fork would take her to her sister. The one straight ahead would take her to the back of the reserve, where the ranger had called the "back nine." She sighed angrily. It was crystal clear that the development would be ripping out trees and paving them with sod for a goddamned golf course. Hesitating, she looked one way, and then another. She didn't have much time left before the shift, and she could hear revelers heading her way. Time to go.

She knew this forest inside and out, backwards and forwards. Every shift felt like home, and she never wanted to leave. Cat clenched her jaw, and padded down the forward fork. Andie was going to get herself killed if she wasn't careful.

CHAPTER FIVE

Andie crept through the woods, her flashlight on a dim setting, just enough to avoid stepping on any branches and snapping them. This time, she had her camera on the right settings, already attached to the tripod for a quick shot, if she could get one. No ranger was going to keep her from at least trying to get a good enough photo to enter, and under the cover of darkness, no one would even know she was there.

She stopped every few steps to listen for rustling that could be a bear, or Cat. If she could just make her way back to that clearing, maybe she'd find her SD card, or see the bear again, though hopefully at a distance. She was vaguely aware of the danger, but she also knew that you had to commit to big risks for great rewards in wildlife photography, especially if you didn't have tens of thousands of dollars in telephoto lenses and the ability to travel to the big reserves or wild areas in other countries. This reserve was her only shot.

Near the clearing, she spotted a tree climb, a seat bolted high up in the tree that hunters often used. It would be a fantastic location to sit and wait for the bear to come back. Bears were creatures of habit, especially this time of year, and especially when it came to food. It's why bear baiting had become such a problem in the larger parks. She frowned, worried that poachers were trying to bait *her* bear.

She climbed up the staples buried deep into the tree's wood, and strapped herself into the seat, detaching the camera from the tripod. It would be too awkward to wield from this vantage point. She slipped the strap back over her shoulder and scanned the dark landscape as best she could, not having night vision goggles or any kind of superpowers. She waited. She checked her phone, (no messages), and turned it off, not wanting to scare any wildlife with an errant buzz or ringtone.

She waited.

The wind blew gently through the trees, waving the bare branches against the rising full moon. An owl hooted somewhere in the distance, much too far to see. They were notoriously difficult to catch, unless you knew where they were nesting. In the summer, this area was rife with bats zig-zagging across sunset skies, but they were all hibernating now. Most of the birds had flown south, and there were fewer deer than in spring. Despite the park's activity in the warmer months, Andie still hadn't managed to capture something good enough to submit. It had to be impressive, something that would make people gasp. It had to be the bear.

The bright, cold light from the end of a flashlight danced through the woods, and Andie pulled her legs up to her chest to hide them from sight as best she could. She was grateful that she was wearing black overalls and a thick black hoodie, the best camouflage for nighttime shoots. She waited for the light to pass, but it just kept sweeping over the same places. Even from her height, Andie could see her own footprints in the mud. Fuck.

"Come on, I know you're out there," Ranger Dade called, rustling the bushes. "The sooner you come out and hand yourself in, the easier this will go."

Andie held her breath.

"I don't have all night, you know. If you make me call in another ranger, we'll just go ahead and refer this to the police, and you'll have to face criminal charges." The ranger shuddered visibly. "Okay, here I go. I'm heading back, now. Calling the police. To arrest you." Ranger Dade shook her head. "For fuck's sake," she muttered under her breath, before climbing back into her ATV. "I'll be back!" she shouted into the darkness. "With police!"

As the vehicle rumbled away, Andie exhaled. That was too close. She wasn't a rule-breaker by nature, and the near miss encounter had her blood pounding in her ears. Getting arrested was the last thing she needed right now. Maybe this was a bad idea. Maybe she should just climb back over the fence and head home, hope that she could capture the bear's picture at first light, when the reserve opened to non-camping members of the public. It would be easier to shoot with better light, anyway.

No.

She'd stay. One good shot and she'd finally have something to enter into the competition. If nothing else, she might be able to see where the bear was going. Adrenaline coursed through her veins, the thrill of the chase when what you were chasing could easily eat you for breakfast. She leaned back in the seat and squinted, scanning the leaf-covered ground, willing the bear to show itself, but there was nothing more than the quiet rustle of underbrush in the November wind.

"Looks like some deer came through here," someone whispered, and a chill crawled up Andie's spine. Poachers. "Rut marks. Betcha we can find them if we keep heading in this direction." The metal of the rifle's barrel glinted in the moonlight, and Andie swallowed hard. Cat had been right.

"Yeah," the other one replied, looking through a night vision scope. "Did you check the trail cam?"

"Not yet." The first one, dressed head to toe in black, stepped up to the base of the tree Andie was hiding in. She was sorely regretting not turning herself in to the ranger, now. At least the ranger didn't have a gun. "Looks like a few came through here, a couple of bucks, too."

"Nice."

"Oh, shit - there's a goddamn bear on this cam!"

The second one snorted back a laugh. "Fuck off, man, there's no bears around here."

"I'm serious, look! It passed through this way last night."

He took the cam and inspected for himself. "Well I'll be goddamned." He sighed loudly. "The boss isn't going to like this. I bet this thing is a protected species or some shit."

"Yeah. Deer are one thing to clear out, but a bear? We're not taking out any bears with rifles this caliber. We'll need, I dunno, a fifty cal, or something."

"Heh. Ever been bear hunting? You sit in a tree stand—"

Andie clutched her legs to her chest and squeezed her eyes shut.

"Hey! There's someone up there!"

"It's a girl!"

"I don't give a shit who it is, we're under strict orders here. If anyone knew about—"

"Shut up, you donkey-brained fuck, we don't need to give her any other ideas." He pointed his rifle at the tree stand. "Why don't you come on out, then?" he asked. "Promise we won't hurt you, we just have to ask a couple of questions."

Andie felt sick. "Fuck off!" she shouted.

"What are you doing out here? You poaching?"

She considered her options. "No."

"Then what the hell are you doing up there?"

"I'm a photographer."

The second man pointed his rifle, too. "Shit, man, I bet she works for the fucking press."

"I'm up here to photograph animals. I'm willing to forget this ever happened, if you just carry on down the path. I won't breathe a word of it."

"Throw down your camera."

She'd just gotten her camera back! "Hell no," she answered. "I didn't take any pictures of you."

"Throw it down, or things will get ugly," the first man said, his finger drifting toward the trigger. "You know what they say about tree stands, dangerous things. Most people don't survive a fall from one of those."

"They'd find the bullet holes, you turkeys."

"Yeah, in a broad that fell out of a tree stand. You can betcha the rangers will chalk it up to a poaching gone wrong. It's no skin off our nose if you live or die."

The second one looked through his scope. "Yeah."

"How do I know you won't just take my camera?" Andie asked.

"What use do I have for a fucking camera?" the second one replied with a laugh. "Come on, babe, just toss it down."

Andie hesitated. "It's an expensive camera."

"What's worth more, the camera or your life?" the first one said. "Don't

38

be stupid, just throw it down." He set the rifle on the ground. "I'll catch it, promise."

"You better," she said, tossing the camera from her perch. Her stomach somersaulted as it flew through the air, until it landed in the man's outstretched hands.

"Thank you." He scanned the empty photo gallery. "Nothing on here. What did you do, delete them?"

"I didn't take any yet, I told you. Been a slow night so far."

The second man kept his rifle trained at her perch. "You looking for that bear?"

"What bear?" Andie lied.

"The fucking *bear*, you two-bit hack," he spat. "What did you do, upload the photos remotely and then delete them off the camera?"

Andie only wished her camera did that. "No, that camera is too old. Only the newer ones do that, and needs some kind of wi-fi, anyway."

"What do you think, man? Do you think she's telling the truth?" the first man said, setting the camera down in the leaves and picking up his rifle. "Or do you think she's bullshitting us?"

"Where did you upload them to?" the second man demanded, his voice growing quieter and more menacing. "Tell us, right now."

"I didn't fucking upload them!" Andie hissed.

The first man pulled the trigger and sent a bullet whizzing past her head. "I said, where—"

A deafening roar came from behind the men, sending them staggering in fright. The bear emerged, dwarfing them in its shadow. It swiped at the first man, knocking the rifle to the ground. Its ears were pinned back, its fur muddy from the wet forest floor. The second man fired wildly at the bear, and missed by a mile. The bear advanced on him, roaring so loud that you could see every deadly tooth. It lashed out at him, its claws easily slicing through his clothes like a hot knife through butter. Even from her height, Andie could see the blood bloom from his skin. He cried out and scrambled backwards, reaching for the gun again.

The bear stepped on the rifle and dragged it away, getting between the men and their weapons. It clamored again, the sound echoing through the trees. The men staggered to their feet and ran further into the woods, calling for help. The bear stared up at the tree stand, where Andie was gripping the seat with white knuckles. "Thank you," she said to the bear, before it tore off after the men.

CHAPTER SIX

Cat sat in the cab of her truck in the parking lot of Jazzy Java, waiting. She had to know if Andie got her camera back, and if she... well, if she found what she'd been looking for. Any reports of bears in that reserve would bring the poachers running, armed to the teeth with huge guns and an agenda - and given the wider population of Applefield wouldn't want bears around, it would be almost impossible to get the authorities to intervene. No one wanted dangerous animals in the park, not where their children played, no matter if the animals just wanted to be left the hell alone. Once they were cleared out, the development would break ground, and rents would skyrocket.

She sighed angrily and smacked her palm against the steering wheel. They'd end up having to move again, she knew it, and this time it would end up being cross-country. It would mean Anita and the boys trying to transfer credits and apprenticeships, it would mean breaking another lease, leaving another place behind. Leaving Andie behind. Cat shook her head, desperate to clear the intrusive thoughts from her mind. Dating should be the furthest thing from her mind, given their almost inevitable forced relocation.

It would be weird to wait outside her apartment, wouldn't it? Yes, it would, and that's why she was sitting in the parking lot, watching cars go in and out, watching for that little blue car. She felt like a stalker. She also felt bad about taking the SD card when she found Andie's camera, but she actually had gotten a photograph of a bear's silhouette. Not crisp enough to sell to a wildlife publication, but enough to get the rangers to start poking around if they saw it, and no one needed that. Guilt sat in her stomach like a brick and made her feel nauseous. This whole thing was stupid, and she was tired of fighting it. She was more tired of perpetually having to restart their lives, though, and that's why she continued to sit, bored out of her mind and exhausted, trying to fake a chance run-in.

Luke said he'd call if Andie stopped in during his shift, but he wasn't the most focused twenty-one-year-old she'd ever met, and if it wasn't a girl he was interested in, he probably wouldn't even look up from the espresso machine. *Boys*, thought Cat, always chasing after some tail. The irony of her own presence in the parking lot, waiting for a girl, did not escape her.

This would be much less complicated if Andie was a man.

Cat closed her eyes for just a moment, feeling the dark relief of her eyelids. Her eyes were always dry after an all-nighter shift. Still, it was the last one until next month. She was achy and weak, like the early signs of a bad flu, but it was just another result of the night shift. She'd be feverish by nighttime, and have to spend the next few days in bed. It wasn't the night shifts that kept her from finishing her nursing practical, it was the several days out of the month having to call in sick, and no employer looked at that favorably, and certainly not in the healthcare professions.

Her eyes still closed, she smacked the steering wheel again to vent the frustration at such an unfair system. She jumped when the horn sounded, and snapped straight in her seat to see Andie, hand on the door of the cafe, staring right at her. Of course. Obviously the second she blinked, she'd show up. This definitely wasn't awkward at all.

Cat grinned stupidly and stumbled out of the car. "Hey, Andie!" she shouted across the parking lot.

"Uh, hey," Andie called back, still holding the door open. "Were you... waiting for me?"

"What? Me? No!" Even to her, it sounded like bullshit. Cat did a weird half-jog to get to the door faster, the heels of her boots scraping against the asphalt.

Andie cocked her head, her brow furrowed. "Are you okay?"

"I'm great!" Cat replied, a little too loudly. *Fucking hell, get it together*, she thought. "I mean, yeah, I'm fine, just a bad night's sleep."

"Stay up too late running away from rangers?"

Cat stared. "What?"

"It's a joke. Because of a couple nights ago..."

"A joke! Right. No, just hung out with my sister, ran some errands, you know." She tugged at the hem of her ribbed sweater dress. "Nothing exciting."

"Are you coming in, or what?" Mara called from the counter. "Cat, nice to see you again - you know Luke isn't off until seven, right?"

"Er—yeah. Just... came in. For a coffee."

Mara raised an eyebrow. "Well that we have. What can I get you?"

Cat hated coffee, in fact. She thought it smelled like burnt garbage, and hated when Luke's work clothes stank up the laundry pile next to the machine. "Just a coffee."

"Drip? Black?"

"...sure?"

"Andie, what about you? We have bear claws in today, I know you like them."

Cat snorted. Of course Andie liked bear claws.

"Yeah please, if you don't mind," Andie said, reaching for her messenger bag. "What do I owe you?"

"Your money is no good here, I told you that. But if you wouldn't mind getting a shot of that cute new reading nook in the corner..."

Andie laughed. "Consider it done." She set her bag on a squashy chair near the bar. "Left my camera in the car, I'll go get it."

Cat perched awkwardly on the arm of the neighboring chair. Why was she acting like such a fool? Shifts made her feel a little loopy, sometimes, but never as bad as this. Mara handed her the coffee, and Cat struggled not to recoil from it. Why anyone drank this crap, she'd never know. She pretended to sip at it politely. "Mm," she said, smiling at Mara. "It's good."

"I've never seen you get a coffee in here. I was starting to think you weren't much of a coffee drinker."

"Oh, I love coffee!" Cat lied. This was getting ridiculous.

"Alright, got it," Andie said as the bells on the door chimed playfully. "Be better with a model, though." She nodded her head at Cat. "Care to be a model

43

for a social media photo?"

"Oh, I don't look very good today, I—"

"I think you look great!" Andie recoiled, her face like a deer caught in someone's high beams. "I just mean, uh—"

Cat sat in the book nook chair. "Alright, I'll do it." She knew she'd be replaying this interaction over and over in her mind later as she shivered underneath two blankets. "How's this?" She presented the coffee in her hand like someone showing off a prize on a game show.

"It's a book nook, how about picking up something to read?" Mara said from the bar, laughing. "Don't overthink it."

"Right." She grabbed a copy of Moby Dick from the shelf and held it up. "How's this?"

"Pick something else," Andie suggested, holding her camera in her hands. "That title would get lots of engagement on social I'm sure Mara doesn't want."

"Oh. Gross." She rifled through the small shelf and chose another one. "How about this illustrated guide to midwestern prairie plants?"

"Perfect. And that's right up your street, too."

"Heh. I guess it is."

Andie held up the camera. "Alright, look engrossed."

"Aye aye, captain," she said, concentrating on the pages. This book was outdated as hell.

The shutter clicked a few times. "That's great. You look very convincing."

"Am I done?"

"Yeah." Andie bit her bottom lip, scrolling through the photos on her camera. Cat stood up and leaned over, trying to see the rest of the gallery, hoping there weren't pictures of bears on there. "Mara, I'll email this to you later, yeah?"

"Sure, sure, whenever you get a chance. Here's your latte and your bear claw." Mara set a brown paper bag and a matching cup on the bar.

"Oh, you're not staying?" Cat asked, unable to disguise the note of disappointment in her voice.

"I've got a work thing."

"I should have suspected, I mean, most people have work in the middle of the morning, don't they?"

"Did you want to talk, or something?"

Cat tucked a tuft of aubergine hair behind her ear. "Just a coincidence again, I guess! I wanted to make sure your camera was okay. You didn't say yesterday."

"Yeah, it's fine, actually. I can't thank you enough for rescuing it, I'd have been totally screwed without it, and water damage repairs would have been almost as much as my rent."

"Well, I assumed it was fine, because you were just using it."

Andie smacked her head with her palm. "Of course. God, you'd think I was the one running on no sleep."

"You're sure it's fine? All the... modes work correctly?"

"All good."

Cat chewed on her lip. "Even the night mode?"

"Yes?"

"And you tried it, just to make sure?" She sounded ridiculous. It would have been easier and less embarrassing at this point to just break into Andie's house and look at the camera herself. "No... problems with the flash or anything?"

"I don't really use a flash for night photography."

"Right. Well, I just wanted to make sure it was okay."

"Thanks." Andie set the camera back into its case. "My SD card from that night went missing, though. Strange as the flap was closed, but I guess anything could have happened when I saw that bear. You didn't find a little card out there did you?"

Cat shrugged, almost performatively. "No." She pretended to take a sip of the coffee, swallowing back a gag. "Still convinced you saw that bear?"

"I'm positive I saw a bear."

Shit. "Why positive?"

Andie zipped up her bag. "I just am."

"Did you see it again?"

"Why do you want to know?"

"Just curious," Cat replied nonchalantly. "You know, if you want, we could

45

hike up the reserve together and look for it."

"I'd actually love that."

"Will you finally believe there are no bears if we search high and low and find nothing?"

"You'll see. Pack your running shoes, lady. Or your climbing shoes. Grizzlies aren't very good at climbing. Did you know that?"

"I did."

"So I'll meet you up there tonight? How about at the fire pit?"

Cat set the coffee down on the table, afraid it was going to make her retch. "Why not at the front gate?"

"Fucking ranger banned me. Sorry, pardon my French."

"I told you they're a bunch of assholes. What did they do, boot you out that next morning?"

"Yup."

"Fuckers."

Andie laughed and sipped her coffee. "You can say that again."

"Alright, I will. They're fuckers. Did you know they're making people sign in now?"

"No. Guess it doesn't matter if you're scaling the fence, though."

"Andie, don't scale the fence."

"Why?"

"Because there's a gap in it closer to the highway. You'll have to park at that old church and walk over, but it's not so bad, and you won't snag your jeans on the barbed wire."

"Something tells me that I'm not the only one who's ever been banned from the reserve."

Cat smirked. "Something tells me you're right."

"How about sunset tonight then, at the gap?"

"It's a date," Cat replied, scribbling her phone number on a napkin and handing it over. "Er—I'll see you there." God, she needed to get some sleep, before she said something *really* stupid. Or something really incriminating.

* * *

Cat leaned against the trunk of an old, knobbed tree, watching the sun go down over the horizon through the trees. The air was crisp and clean, just the way she liked it, and when she breathed, clouds floated from her lips. Her stomach flip-flopped in anticipation of seeing Andie, or maybe it was nervousness about running into the ranger again. Maybe it was both.

The gap in the fence was well hidden, cloaked behind a patch of convenient pine trees, their thick boughs obscuring where the barbed wire lay rusted and cut on the cold ground. It would frost overnight, she could feel it in the air, that wintery snap that blew through the wind. It wouldn't be long before the big houses behind her put up elaborate displays of Christmas lights, each one trying to outdo the rest, running up exorbitant electric bills. It wasn't like Cat to feel like such a miser this time of year, but their impending move had her feeling sour. Some of the folks in those mansions could do with a visit from the Ghost of Christmas Past, if you asked her.

She watched the path that led up to the old churchyard, waiting for Andie to appear. She knew she shouldn't have come so early. She looked like some kind of obsessive weirdo just waiting there like that. Cars drove by on the nearby road, most of them going much too fast considering the temperature. Black ice was a hell of a way to go, and it would be rife on the streets after the damp weather. Cat checked her phone again, continuing to ignore the messages from her sister wanting to know every detail about her... well, it wasn't a date, not really.

Unless it was.

No. Definitely not a date. Andie didn't seem like the type that would be interested in her. She shouldn't be getting all roped into something, anyway. Not when they'd be moving across the country again in a couple of months.

Still, there was no rule saying she shouldn't have fun while she could...

"Argh!" she grunted to herself. It wasn't like her to get hung up on a stranger, yet here she was, waiting to break into a park reserve. Like a complete freak.

"Cat!" Andie called, waving through the arch of trees that lined the path, her pale cheeks already rosy from the cold.

"Hey, you ready?"

Andie held up her camera, already attached to an expensive looking tripod. "Hell yeah."

"I don't know why you're so excited, we're not going to see anything."

"You never know."

"If we run into anything out of the ordinary, it's more likely to be poachers than a bear."

Andie's face faltered. "I hope we don't see any poachers."

"I've got a mean right hook, you're safe with me." It was the truth. Mostly.

"And if we do find a bear, are you going to punch that, too?"

Cat laughed. "Hell no. I'll climb the nearest tree and hope it doesn't eat your camera for dinner." She sobered, pushing away the pine branches. "We won't see any bears, though."

"Do you want to bet on that?" Andie asked, stepping over the cut fence.

"Alright, Camera Girl, let's make it interesting, then. What's your wager?"

For a moment, the only sound was their boots crunching against freezing leaves. "A date." Cat choked on her own saliva, and had to stop to cough up what felt like half a lung. For fuck's sake, could she be any more awkward? Andie turned back, chewing her bottom lip. "Are you okay?"

"I'm fine," Cat replied, her voice coarse and her eyes watering. "A date, huh?"

"I'm sorry," Andie said, covering her face. "I obviously misread things, and—"

"No, you're on. If we see a bear, we go on a date."

"You realize that we're not leaving this reserve until I find one now, right?"

"We'll see about that. Come on, let's go."

"And what if we don't see one? What's *your* wager?"

Cat climbed over a felled tree, the denim of her jeans scraping against the damp bark. "You convince Mara to make something other than coffee. I can't stand that stuff."

Andie burst out laughing. "I knew something was up earlier, you looked like you were holding a cup of nuclear waste."

"Was it that obvious?"

"Not in the photo. In that you're... very convincing. You look like a genuine hipster."

"Oh God, don't tell me that," Cat said with a snort. "It will ruin all of my credibility with the mainstream tea drinkers."

"Mara already offers teas."

"I don't like tea, either."

"Then what *do* you like?"

"It's silly."

"It can't be that weird, just tell me."

"Hot chocolate, the good stuff, and extra marshmallows."

Andie squinted into the growing darkness. "I think the clearing is this way," she said, shimmying between two close-growing trees. "What do you mean by 'the good stuff?'"

"None of that boxed crap. It has to be the kind made slow, with real chocolate."

"Well you're a woman with taste, clearly."

"Hey, you asked."

"Alright, it's a deal. No bears, I'll see what I can do to talk Mara into making good hot chocolate. I'm warning you, though, that woman has a serious passion for coffee beans. It's like an obsession. She never gives up on sourcing the best stuff available."

"While I admire her dedication, I'm sorry to report that it all tastes like garbage water to me," Cat said, drawing them back towards the path she knew led to the clearing.

"Are you sure you're going the right way?"

"Yeah, I think so."

"I did some research on the history of bears in this area, did you know that there were two grizzly bear sightings last year?"

Cat stopped dead in her tracks, her blood ice in her veins. "What?"

"Yeah, a couple people who came in to take pictures saw one near dawn, and the other time it was some teenagers smoking weed in some makeshift fort."

"Bears."

"Yeah, bears. Big ones, too, they reckon probably three hundred pounds."

"Weird that no one would report on that."

Andie shrugged, heading deeper into the forest. "Rangers deemed it an impossibility, no one followed up. But I've seen it. I know it's here."

"You realize bears can travel a long way for food? And wouldn't most be hibernating?" Cat had to work hard to keep her tone even and casual.

"This is the only reserve big enough for a long ways, and people probably would have seen a huge bear wandering along the interstate. And they usually head in to hibernate in late November, so we'd be right on schedule to see one preparing."

"Isn't that when they're most dangerous?"

"Yeah."

"And you aren't, I dunno, scared?"

"You should know something about me, Cat. I will probably die trying to pet something deadly because it's cute."

That might turn out to be true, if things went badly.

"Anyway," Andie continued, "even if I just get an honorable mention in this wildlife photography competition, it could open a lot of doors for me. Funding. Equipment."

"You seem like you have a lot of gear already."

Andie shot her a look. "Are you kidding? This camera is already four years out of date. I barely have any decent zoom lenses, nothing like some of the professionals use—"

"Okay, okay. Clearly, I know nothing about photography equipment."

"It's okay, I don't know anything about rare plants."

"A knowledge of necessity. Sometimes cutting down a forest can be halted if you can prove there's an endangered species there." Cat kicked a rock across the path, and heard it bounce into the bushes. It was getting dark. "For a while, anyway. Until poachers or hired thugs come in and clear it out. No proof of habitation, no construction delay."

"Hmm..." Andie mumbled.

"What?"

"Thinking."

"About huge, man-eating bears?"

"If they're man-eating, I think we're safe, being women and all."

"Very funny."

Andie pushed her way into the small clearing and turned on her flashlight. "Don't worry, I won't quit my day job."

"So how long are you prepared to wait for your bear?"

"All night."

"Until dawn?"

"If I have to."

"You know," Cat said, "we could always abandon this mission and go get pancakes at that diner at the corner of—"

"I know you're kidding, but this is important to me."

"Alright, let's wait for a bear."

Andie sat on a felled log and arranged her tripod. "We should probably stay quiet."

Cat mimed zipping her lips and joined her on the log. It was going to be a long night. Maybe once the sun rose, she could convince Andie to go get some breakfast. Her stomach growled at the thought, and she cursed herself for not packing a goddamn snack. Being hungry made her feel on edge.

"Here," Andie whispered, handing over a brownie in plastic wrap. "You can eat this."

"You brought food?"

"Please, it's not my first stakeout. I once spent almost an entire week trying to capture a long-eared bat." Andie examined the settings on her camera. "Besides, I saw you eat all my food the first night I met you, I know to come prepared."

Cat bit into the brownie, and it was the best thing she'd ever eaten this deep into the forest. Deep, fudgy, the perfect texture, moist, she could eat a whole tray of them, if left unsupervised. "Did you want any?" she asked, eyeing up the last bite.

"No."

"Are you sure—"

"Shh."

Someone was approaching, someone quiet. Trained to be quiet. Cat's breath slowed, and she focused on where it was coming from. Poachers.

CHAPTER SEVEN

Panic gripped the base of Andie's skull, her innate fight-or-flight instincts grappling for superiority. "Did you hear that?" she whispered. Beside her, Cat nodded. *Poachers*, she mouthed. Andie turned off her flashlight and set the camera to record. This time, she'd get them on camera.

The footsteps approached carefully, barely audible over the sound of the wind whistling through the trees. With each step came a pause, just long enough that she'd start to question if she'd even heard anything at all. They came closer, just to the other side of the copse that lined the clearing. Andie squinted into the darkness and found herself reaching for Cat's hand, but it wasn't there.

"Don't move," Cat hissed, moving silently to the center of the clearing.

"Wait—"

"I mean it."

Andie stood, keeping one hand looped through the camera strap. If she had to run again, she didn't want to lose her camera.

A small bear, much scrawnier than the other one she'd seen, wandered into the moonlight, heading straight for Cat. Wanting to scream a warning, Andie's breath caught in her throat, and none of her limbs would cooperate. Fear coursed through her veins like poison.

"Who are you?" Cat demanded, staring down the bear, hands on her hips. "Don't piss me off."

Why the hell is she talking to a bear? She's going to get herself killed, Andie thought, shaking her head to wake up from the dream. She positioned the camera, but Cat was standing in front of the bear, blocking the shot.

"Get out of here. Don't come back."

The bear roared, but instead of sounding threatening, it just sounded kind of sad. It approached Cat and laid down on the ground, its face in the dirt.

"What in the f—" Cat said, before dodging out of the way of a huge dart. "Andie!" she shouted. "Poachers!"

Andie leaped up off the felled tree and snatched at the camera, collapsing the tripod legs as she ran. She wished she had a stabilizer, this footage was going to be a mess. She zoomed into the gaps between the trees, hunting for faces amid the sparse foliage.

"There!" Cat shouted, pushing the bear that didn't want to move, pointing to the other side.

Andie spun, looking for the poacher. She caught the flash of a gun barrel, and behind it, a black mask and a knitted hat. Zooming in, she held the camera as still as she could in her trembling hands. It would be a miracle if any of this footage was usable. She glanced over her shoulder, and Cat was still pushing the motionless bear. "Cat! It's been tranquilized!" Despite the darkness, a large, silver needle glinted, protruding from the bear's leg.

The muzzle of the gun flashed, and Andie dropped to the ground, rolling back into the bushes. Her heart pounded fiercely in her chest, her fingers searching for the camera. It was their only chance at catching these assholes on film - her phone was seven years old, and the lens had been cracked for three. Every spare cent she made went towards her gear.

"Fuck off!" Cat shouted, standing in front of the sleeping bear, guarding it. "Leave her alone!"

"We don't want to hurt it," the masked man said, loading another round into the rifle. "This reserve isn't big enough for a bear. We're relocating it."

"The hell you are."

"Listen, lady, just back away, alright? We've got jobs to do."

Cat stood firm, her hands balled into fists at her sides. "I'm warning you. Back off."

The man laughed. "What are you going to do, slap us?"

"Prick," Andie muttered under her breath, her fingers closing around the camera strap and pulling it to her chest. She pressed the record button. The man was small in the frame, as though he wasn't nearly six feet tall, dwarfing Cat's small stature.

He waved her away again. "This bear is staying right here until you can produce the wildlife trust paperwork that affirms what you're doing here."

"You're trying my patience."

"And you're pissing me off. There are poachers crawling all over these woods nowadays, and I'm not going to stand by and watch you cart off a bear without the proper authorization."

"Who are you to tell me what to do, a ranger?" he scoffed. "Move away from the bear."

Another man stepped into the clearing, the same as the night before. Andie stifled a gasp. "Come on, man, the transport is waiting. What the hell are you waiting for?"

"She's in the way!" the first man protested, gesturing at Cat. "I'm not about to shoot a human, even if it is just a tranq."

"I don't give a shit about this hippie tree-hugger bullcrap. Shoot her and let's go."

Cat dropped her jacket to the ground. "This is your last warning to get the hell out of here before things get ugly."

"Fuck this," the man said, and raised the rifle to his shoulder. Andie leaped out of the bushes and caught him around the knees, sending the gun flying into the darkness.

"Another one!" the second man said, kicking her square in the stomach. Pain exploded through her body, her lungs useless and breathless. She rolled over, clutching her torso, moaning in pain. At least the camera was still recording, the tiny, blinking red dot flashing behind the foliage.

"Grab its legs," the first one said, shoving Cat out of the way. "It's a scrawny one, and not far to the truck."

Andie's vision was clouded with pain, but when Cat bent double, fur sprouting from every inch of bare skin, she knew she wasn't seeing things, but she pinched herself just to make sure she wasn't dreaming. In the dim light of the moon, Cat's shirt and jeans popped at the seams as she grew exponentially in size, her face lengthening into a snout until she was a full-sized grizzly, roaring into the faces of the terrified men. She swiped at one, and then the other, her dangerous claws drawing blood beneath their insufficient tactical gear. They screamed. The bear bellowed, tossing them around like rag dolls, throwing one into the trunk of an old tree, and the other into the bushes.

One of the masked men reached for the tranquilizer gun, but Andie kicked it out of his reach, her boot connecting with his kneecap. He grunted and grabbed for it again. This time the bear - Cat? - ripped at his clothing, threatening to sink her teeth into the meat of his arm.

"Call for backup!" the one in the bushes yelled. "They never said there'd be *two* bears out here!"

"Get to the truck! It's gonna kill us both!"

The bear roared again, sending threatening echoes around the cold, dark forest. The men stumbled, and ran, the bear screaming after them until their footsteps had faded down the path.

"Cat?" Andie asked cautiously.

The bear crashed into the bushes, out of sight, its huge paws heavy on the crispy, iced leaves on the ground of the park.

"Hey, be careful—"

The crunch of the glass made Andie feel even sicker than the boot to the guts. She knew that it was her camera, crushed beneath the immense weight of the grizzly. No amount of money would be able to cover the repairs on smashed lenses and mirrors. It would be a write off. "Hey," she repeated sadly.

In the quiet, the sound of the shift was clearer - bones popping the way they would during an intense pilates session, and the soft ripple of fur on skin. "Cat?"

"Check on that bear, see if she's alright."

"Is she—like you?"

"Yeah."

Andie knelt over the unconscious bear, one arm still clutching her stomach. "It's breathing. I think it's just sleeping."

"Can you toss me something to put on? It's cold."

"Um..." The clothes were all but torn to shreds, ripped apart by the bear's expansion. "Here," she said, tossing her own coat into the brush. "I think your stuff is ruined."

"Fuck. See, this is why I don't wear stuff I like into this damn reserve. What about my jeans?"

"I don't know how salvageable they are."

"Well I can't exactly go walking around half naked!"

"There's something hanging from a tree over here—"

Cat rustled in the bushes. "Probably this bear's cache. Grab it."

"Uh, pair of sneakers, a sports bra... here we go, sweatpants." She tossed them into the bushes, along with the shoes. She hadn't seen where Cat's went. "What about the bear?"

"She'll stay like this until she wakes up. We need to get her out of here, before those fucks come back." Cat squinted in the dark. "Where's your camera?"

"You, uh..." Andie bent and retrieved the camera, confirming her worst fears. It was completely and totally ruined, spider-webbed cracks across the lens, which had separated from the body, leaving behind a shattered screen and electrics severed from the rest of it. She shoved the pieces into her bag, which was still secured across her torso.

"Oh my God, I'm so sorry. I didn't even see it, I'm not that... aware, when I'm shifted."

"It's okay," Andie said in a small voice, even though it very much was not okay. "Let's get the bear somewhere safe."

"We'll take her to my house, we can sneak her in under a tarp."

"What if your landlord sees?"

Cat snorted, tying the shoelaces of the borrowed sneakers. "What's he gonna do, keep my security deposit? I'm pretty sure he decided on that the day we moved in."

"Might charge you pet rent."

"I wouldn't put it past him, to be honest." Cat patted the bear gently on the head. "I hope you're strong, Andie. Grab her feet, I bet we can gently drag her to the gap in the fence."

"Then what?"

"I'm texting my sister to bring the truck down. She'll understand."

Even as a small, underweight bear, it was almost too much weight for the both of them to shift. Sleeping bears weren't exactly cooperative, so when two young guys bounded down the path and grabbed a paw each, she was grateful - especially when she recognized one of them as Luke, a barista at Jazzy Java.

"We live with Cat," one of them explained. He looked sideways. "Does she know?"

Cat nodded solemnly. "It couldn't be helped, those poachers were about to take this bear."

"Shit," Luke said. "Never thought *you'd* be the one to break the cardinal rule." He nodded at the sleeping bear they were all carrying. "Do we know her?"

"No. She doesn't look familiar."

"That's a big risk to take on a stranger."

"Yeah, well, I'd hope that another werebear would take pity on you knuckleheads if you ever got into trouble." She sighed and shifted the bear's weight in her grip. "And that's seeming more and more likely these days."

They sidled through the gap in the fence and set the bear on the truck bed, covering her with a large blue tarp, weighted down on the sides with paving bricks. The boys went to climb into the back seat, and the young woman driving stuck her head out of the driver's side window. "Nuh uh! Let Cat and... whoever that is, ride. You guys can walk."

"We can fit!" Luke said, squishing himself against the door. "See?"

"There's a frigging *bear* in the bed of the truck. I don't think risking getting pulled over is a great plan."

"Come on, Anita, please?"

"No!" She tossed a five-dollar bill out the window. "Walk home through town, pick up some burgers. Cat and whoever that bear is are going to need it."

"Okay, but I'm getting fries," Luke grumbled, setting off down the path.

Andie climbed in the back seat and buckled her seat belt. This night was definitely not what she'd expected.

"Nice to meet you," Anita said, turning around in her seat to offer a handshake. "Are you my sister's new girlfriend, or something?"

"Nita!" Cat hissed, gently slapping her arm away. "Just drive, will you?"

"Fine, fine." She drove across the field behind the churchyard, the truck bouncing over every uneven mole hill and divet from the teenagers riding ATVs. "I hope he gets me some chicken nuggets," she mumbled.

"Thanks for picking us up," Cat said, staring out the window, on high alert.

"Not like you gave me much of a choice sending a message like that. Until the boys crashed in, I thought it was one of them you'd found in the woods. Do we even know this bear?"

"No. I don't think so, anyway."

"You back there," Anita said, looking at Andie from the rear-view mirror. "You see anything... weird?"

"I saw your sister turn into a bear, if you'd consider that weird."

"Well, I mean, it's not weird for *me*, but yeah. Sure."

Andie looked back at the tarp in the bed of the truck. "So, are you all... like that?"

The turn signal ticked, the light flashing against the car in front of them at the stop sign. "Yeah," Cat said, finally. "But you can't say anything. To anyone."

"I don't think anyone would believe me, even if I did. But no, of course I won't." She picked at the blister on her palm. "So you're like... werewolves?"

"Ugh, *no*," Anita spat, making a disgusted face. "There's a reason everyone knows about werewolves, and it's not because they're careful and level-headed. Bunch of prima donnas if you ask me."

"We have a little more control over shifts. And we're less likely to be pompous assholes." Cat rubbed at her temples. "I'm getting a headache already."

"Alright, we're almost home," Anita soothed. "The boys will bring food, you should eat before you crash out."

"So you can... choose when you shift?"

Cat shifted in her seat. "Kind of. We have to shift during the full moon, or we get sick with what's basically a really terrible flu. It can kill you if you're not careful, and it's hard to suppress the shift. We can choose to shift when it's not a full moon, like I did tonight, but it takes a toll. I'll be laid up for a few days, at least."

"How have you stayed hidden?"

"Andie, listen, I know this is probably a lot for you right now, but we've got a bear in the back and my sister is about to have the mother of all migraines. Maybe we can hold off on the full history of the Weres for now?"

"Right. Sure."

The headlights flashed against the driveway when they pulled in, and Anita jumped out, snatching the keys from the ignition. "Let's get her inside," she whispered, gesturing towards the tarp. "Keep her wrapped up in that, in case the neighbors get home."

Andie nodded, grasping one end of the tarp and lowering it gently to the ground from the truck. Even the thick plastic made it easier to move the bear than trying to grasp her huge paws without hurting her. They went to the back door, and slid the bear inside before untying the tarp, after Cat pulled the curtains on every window in the house.

"What now?" Anita asked, nudging the bear with the toe of her shoe.

"Wait for her to wake up."

"And then what?"

Cat sighed and sat in one of the chairs, rubbing her temples. "Figure out why the hell she launched herself at me in the reserve, and what she was doing there to begin with. As far as I knew, we were the only ones for at least two hundred miles, maybe more if that group in Missouri moved on."

"You should have something to drink, Catriona."

"The boys will be here soon, I can wait."

Anita yanked a generic brand sports drink from the wobbly refrigerator. "Nuh uh. Drink this before it gets any worse."

"Is she going to be... okay?" Andie asked, still not totally convinced she wasn't having the strangest dream of her life.

"I'm fine, I'll just be a little under the weather for a few days." She already looked paler than she should, and the light sheen of sweat glistened in the yellow light from the bare bulb that hung from the ceiling. "Shifting outside of the natural cycle wreaks some havoc on us, we're not sure why."

"How long do you think this bear will sleep?" Anita asked.

"She's scrawny. Hasn't been eating enough for the autumn metabolic shift. I doubt we'll see her awake before the morning, at least." Cat laid her head on her arms on the table. "Nita, why don't you go pick up the boys in town? Take the extra five from the jar and get a little extra. When this bear wakes up, we should fatten her up."

"I don't want to leave you here on your own."

"I'm not alone, Andie is here."

Anita gave her a withering look. "If you're sure you're okay here with the Normie."

"Anita."

"Fine." She took the keys from the hook and closed the front door behind her, the engine of the truck roaring into life a moment later.

"You okay?" Cat asked. "I know this is all... kind of a lot."

"I'm not completely convinced that this isn't all a very elaborate and convincing hallucination, to be honest."

"I hope I didn't scare you."

Andie shifted in her seat. "No. It was pretty cool, actually."

"Wow, you really are a wildlife photographer at heart, aren't you?"

"Heh."

"I'm sorry again about your camera, really."

"It was an accident."

Cat looked down at her shoes. "Yeah." She took a deep swig of the sport drink and finished by wiping her mouth with the back of her hand. "Any chance it could get repaired?"

"No." The shards in her bag made her feel sick. No more contract work to help pay the rent. Maybe she could get some extra work, not that this town ever had any spare work to be had. She felt like she was watching her dream disappear into thin air in real time.

"What about the storage card you had in there? Would you still have footage of those poachers?"

"It snapped."

"Oh." Cat ran her fingers through her short, cropped hair. "Andie, I—"

The truck pulled back into the driveway, and Cat's sister and the boys piled into the kitchen with steaming bags of food that they slid across the table to Cat. "Got eight burgers, a fry for Luke, and chicken for Anita."

"Thanks."

"You should eat at least two tonight, but three would be better," Anita added. "You're already going to feel like shit in the morning, don't make it worse."

"Alright! I'm eating!" Cat shot back, unwrapping the first one.

Andie's stomach rumbled, and she coughed to cover up the sound, vowing to get herself something on the way home from this whole mess. A double cheeseburger with extra pickles, a large fry, and a cookie, if her bank account allowed it. She deserved it for not freaking the hell out tonight.

Felix moved to steal a fry, and Luke swatted him away. "Fuck off, it was my idea!"

"Boys," Anita warned, pushing the bottle of sport drink at Cat again. "You need some more."

"I'm tired," Cat announced halfway through the third hamburger, ketchup smeared on her cheek. She swayed in her chair, her eyes closed as she yawned. "I can't stay up much later."

"I'll help," Andie offered, eager to get one more moment with Cat before she left.

"I'm her sister, I'll help," Anita said, stepping between them.

Cat wobbled to her feet. "Relax, Nita. I have to give her the jacket back, anyway. C'mon Andie," she beckoned. "Last door on the right." She snorted. "In our palatial residence, it would be easy to get lost."

Her room was small and cramped, but clean and organized, with a small shoe rack in the open front closet displaying two pairs of boots and some bunny slippers, and dresses hung in color order from the rail. The window let in a draft, but she didn't seem to mind, even though Andie shivered.

"Turn around so I can take off the jacket."

Andie obeyed, fixing her eyes on a framed picture of all the Bears on the wall, their arms around each other outside what looked like a theme park. When the jacket landed on her shoulder, she asked, "Can I turn around now?"

"Yeah." Cat was pulling on some worn, green, fluffy socks over her pajamas.

"You have bears on your pajamas?"

"Kind of an in-joke."

"I hope you feel better soon."

Cat sat on the edge of her bed. "I will. I wasn't shifted too long, and we're just past the full moon."

"What happens if you shift for too long?" Andie asked. "Sorry. Too many questions."

"Honestly, we don't even have all the answers about our kind. We know it's genetic, hereditary."

"So if you bit me…?"

"Then I'd probably recommend you get medical attention, so it didn't get infected, but no, you wouldn't become a Bear."

"Hmm." Andie fidgeted with the brass buckle on the strap of her bag. "I guess we should get you tucked in, then."

Cat yawned. "That sounds excellent." She shimmied beneath the covers, punching her pillow into shape. Andie wished she could snuggle in next to her, make her a hearty breakfast in the morning.

"You owe me a date, you know."

"I don't know about that, you never said anything about seeing *two* bears."

"See, in my mind, that just means I get two dates."

"Alright, Andie. Two dates it is. But next time, I don't want to be in my pajamas."

"I don't think we'll be needing pajamas." Andie blushed a deep crimson. "I just mean, we'd be out doing something fun, not—goodnight, Cat."

"Night." She turned over, and Andie hit the light switch on her way out of the room, pulling the door closed.

Everyone else was still in the kitchen, gathered around the bear. "I guess I'll be going now, if someone could give me a lift back to my car? I'm parked at the old churchyard, it's okay if you can't, I'll just walk."

Anita narrowed her eyes. "I don't know if that's such a good idea. Not after what you saw tonight, we have to be careful, you know."

"I won't say anything."

"How can we be sure?"

"I promise!"

"We don't know you, Andie. You could march right on out of here and straight up to the sheriff's office."

Andie barked out a laugh. "With what proof? They'd be far more likely to lock me up in the drunk tank than believe me."

"Aren't you a photographer or something?"

"My camera got smashed."

Anita leaned back in her chair and heaved out a sigh. "Okay." She wrapped up the remaining burgers and set them back in the bag. "I guess if Cat had wanted you to stay, she would have said so."

"One rule for her, and a different one for us," Felix grumbled.

"We're all flying by the seat of our pants here, Felix, can you not?" Anita said. She tossed him the keys. "Give her a ride to her car. With those poachers wandering around, we don't want them to pick her up."

"Is that something they would do?" Andie asked. "Given I'm not a... a Bear?"

"Don't put anything past them," Felix agreed. "They'd do anything to get what they want. Come on, I'll take you to your car, and I'll make sure you get home okay."

* * *

When Andie got home, she dumped the remains of her camera out onto the table, and cried.

CHAPTER EIGHT

Cat wandered into the kitchen the next morning, feeling groggy and sick. It was like a hangover, but without all the fun that preceded it. Her head pounded, and her stomach lurched angrily.

"Finally, it's almost noon," her sister chided, frying some eggs. "Our guest is still asleep, but the boys moved her to the living room where she'll be a little warmer."

"I feel like shit."

"Yeah, we all knew that would happen. Well, all of us except Andie, that is." Anita slid the eggs onto a plate that was already loaded with heavily buttered bread and cheap sausage links. "Do you want to explain why you let her just waltz out of here last night?"

"Do we have any juice?"

"In the fridge. Don't avoid the question, Catriona."

"She won't say anything."

"And how the hell do you know that?"

Cat drank the orange juice straight from the carton and tossed the emptied container into the trash. "I just know."

"She's a *photographer*. And a broke one, at that. She could be laughing her way all the way to the bank this morning."

"She doesn't have any evidence. Her camera is broken."

"Well, that's what she *says*, but—"

"I'm the one who broke it. I made sure there was no evidence." Just saying the words out loud made the guilt that seeded in her gut the night before bloom into regret.

"Oh."

"And I really like her, too, so I just... it sucks."

Anita set the plate in front of Cat. "You should eat."

"I'm not hungry."

"Stop being stubborn, you know you'll feel worse if you don't."

"I feel bad."

"You always said things could never work out long term with a Normie."

Cat stabbed the yolk of her eggs with a fork, letting the golden ooze spread across the plate. "Maybe I'm just tired of being alone. It would be nice to build a life with someone, you know, and the Bears we've met... well, they've left a lot to be desired."

"Yeah, remember that one Bear out in Colorado? What was her name again?"

"Ugh, don't," Cat said with a laugh. "What a disaster." She nibbled the end of a sausage before shoving the whole thing in her mouth. Her sister was right, as usual. "Andie just seems really sweet. And she's cute, and—"

"Are you *smitten?*"

Cat threw a bread crust at her. "Shut up!"

"Does she like you?"

"She asked me on a date."

"Are you gonna go?"

"Yeah."

"Well," Anita said, sitting down with her own plate of food, "just be careful. Isn't that what you always tell us? You've practically burned it into our brains."

"I just want to keep you safe."

"Yeah, well, what do you think I'm trying to do?"

"I know." Cat folded a piece of toast in half, using it to soak up the yolk. "I don't want to move, Nita. And it's not just this thing with Andie, either, I just... I want us all to be able to build a life somewhere. I'm damn tired of running."

"What are the odds this development gets canceled?"

"With Syndicorp? Slim to none."

"What if we... intervened?"

Cat raised an eyebrow. "I'm listening."

"We involve the local hippie tree-huggers, tell them there are bears in the reserve and that the development would cause problems, and—"

"No." Cat shook her head. "That will draw in poachers from all over the damn place, looking for a trophy and a nice kickback from Syndicorp. It's too dangerous."

"But imagine if it got statewide attention—"

"Anita, for God's sake, attention is the last thing we want!"

"The Wolves did it in Yellowstone!"

"Yeah, well, it's a lot easier to endear the general public to something that looks a little like their puppy. If folks around here about bears holing up in the park, they'll start petitioning for relocation, and then what? Besides, we'd have to be night shifting outside the cycle to keep people interested and—" she interrupted herself with a loud sneeze. "And obviously, that takes a toll."

"If it let us stay, though?"

"We don't even know about that Bear in the living room yet. We should just chill out until we know what that's all about."

Anita pushed a sausage around on her plate. "What if she's from some secret government organization?"

"Then we've got bigger problems than a housing development, that's for sure."

"Do you think they might have found us?"

"I mean, it's not impossible, is it? We do our best to lay low, but who knows how much those secretive shits know about us."

"I'm not going without a fight."

Cat laid a hand on her sister's arm. "We don't know if that's the case, yet. She might just be a wayward Bear passing through."

"You realize that might be a Cub in there? What then? If she ran from another den, they could show up here and claim her."

"There aren't any dens around here, Nita. We'd have heard if someone went missing."

"At least the boys are of age now. No one can claim them, either."

"I'm not sure their parents even cared. Ours didn't."

"Hi." A girl, probably about fourteen years old, stood in the doorway of the kitchen, wrapped in the blanket from the couch.

Cat looked at Anita. "Shit."

* * *

Andie laid on her rumpled bed and stared at the ceiling. She hadn't slept, even after the previous night's overwhelm. Cat was a Bear. Werebears were real, and apparently, so were Werewolves. What else was real? Vampires? Ghosts? Mermaids?

Daisy was asleep in her cage, nestled into the soft bedding. She hadn't been pleased that Andie came home so late, and ate her dinner as sullenly as a chinchilla could. Were there Werechinchillas, too? Weredolphins? Were... beetles? Andie shook her head. This was all too much. She wished she could go back to yesterday afternoon, before she learned that the woman she'd been crushing on turned into a three-hundred pound grizzly a few times a month. Sometimes, dating was like trying to fish in a lake of piranhas. If they weren't secret republicans, they were secret cryptids, apparently.

She checked her phone again, hoping for a message from Cat, despite everything. No messages. The sun was already starting to set, and she'd been awake well over twenty-four hours. She blinked furiously, trying to clear the sleep shadows in her peripheral view. Maybe a cup of tea would help. If she didn't get some sleep, then work tomorrow was going to suck even more than it was already going to, having to explain why she'd have to sign out equipment before every shift now, taking access away from the desk clerks who sometimes needed the cameras to document progress for the investors.

Her broken camera was still spread out on the table where she'd left it, and now the shattered lens glimmered in the golden hour light. It was poetic, and if she had another camera, she'd take a picture. But she didn't. Even the storage card was broken, having been snapped in half. There was no record of the poachers, or of Cat turning into a huge bear. The camera repair store confirmed her worst fears that morning when she called the store to explain. Her camera was too old, and the parts and labor too expensive, to merit a repair. They unhelpfully recommended a refurbished camera from their stocks. A maxed out credit card and an empty bank account weren't going to pay the hundreds it would cost for a replacement.

The blankets tangled around her legs, and she kicked them off onto the threadbare rug on the floor. She was too restless. The kitchen in her studio apartment was small, but functional, as long as you weren't trying to make anything too fancy. Andie filled the kettle and set it on top of the electric burner, and leaned against the narrow counter top, waiting for the shrill whistle to indicate the water had boiled. She held an empty mug in her hands as though it was full, the flimsy tea bag string draped over the side. Chamomile would help her relax, it always did. But then, she'd never seen a Werebear before, either.

Water poured into the mug and tinged yellow, the steam floating up to the ceiling in delicate curls. She set the mug on the table and deposited fresh hay into Daisy's cage. "Do you want to have some playtime?" she asked, almost expecting the chinchilla to answer. After last night, nothing would surprise her. Daisy continued to sleep, not ready to wake up yet. "Lazy Daisy," Andie said with a smirk.

She shoved her feet into a pair of boots by the door and ran down to the ground floor to check the mail, finding two ominous looking FINAL NOTICE letters inside her box. One from the credit card company, and one from the electric company, threatening to turn off her lights if she didn't pay up by the end of the week.

"For fuck's sake," Andie muttered, trudging back up the stairs. "What next?"

* * *

"Okay, let's lay this all out on the line," Cat said to the girl, who was now freshly showered and squeezed into one of the boys' tracksuits. They'd have to get her something else. "Start at the beginning."

The girl took a deep breath. "My name is Delilah. I went to the park to find something to eat. I thought I smelled something familiar. I guess maybe I did."

"Who sent you?" Anita asked, a hard edge to her tone.

"No one sent me."

"Then how do you know who we are?"

Cat pushed the leftover burgers at Delilah. "Eat, I know you're probably feeling as crappy as I am right now."

"I grew up in the foster system," she said between bites. "Last year, I—"

"You shifted for the first time, didn't you?" Anita prompted.

Delilah nodded. "Yeah. Except I didn't know what was happening, and my foster parents saw. They freaked out. Said I was some kind of demon come to punish them, they kicked me out that same night."

"I'm sorry," Cat said.

"I jumped on a freight car headed east, stealing what I could. Ended up in New England."

The tension in Cat's muscles eased, and she sat back in her chair. "And then what?"

"I tried to find work. Couldn't. Too young, they said. I kept trying to refuse to shift, it hurt. I thought I was some kind of freak. I was scared."

"I don't like this," Anita announced. "This could be some kind of a ploy. She could be a spy, leading some kind of secret agents straight to us."

"No, I'm not a spy! I was hopping the freight trains, I stopped off nearby to try and scavenge some food, I—I felt drawn to the woods, like I'd find answers there."

"You've never met another Bear?" Cat demanded. "You don't know anything about what you are?"

Delilah shook her head. "No. I spent months looking, in every park that had bear sightings. I ran into some Wolves in Yellowstone, they said no Bears were allowed in the park."

"Unsurprising," Anita muttered. "Bunch of elitist rednecks."

"I just kept looking, and I ended up here."

"Pretty convenient that I found you at exactly the right moment. You'd be in some lab by now, being poked and prodded."

"Are you working for them?" Anita asked. "Syndicorp, or... you know. The government?"

"Nita, she's like, thirteen."

"I'm fourteen," Delilah announced proudly. "And I'm not working for anyone, I just—I didn't know where else to go. I've been spending every moon hiding in abandoned farm buildings, or empty parking garages. Last time was the first time I spent one in a forest, and... well, you can see how that turned out."

"When did you shift? Before or after they found you?"

"After. I was sleeping in an old tent I found, and I heard them creeping around. I ran out, hid my stuff in a cache as soon as I felt the shift coming. I was so scared, I couldn't stop it.

"Control will come, in time," Cat explained. "With practice."

"Catriona, you're not seriously letting her stay here, are you?"

"Well, we can't just throw her out on the street, can we?"

Anita scoffed. "Why not? She could be reporting everything back to *them*."

"I don't even have a phone," Delilah shot back.

Cat closed her eyes against the painful, pulsating light of day. "Let's all just take a breath, shall we? Two out of the three of us aren't exactly in good form today. My patience is paper thin right now, and I'm not in the mood to argue."

Delilah's eyes filled with tears and spilled out onto her adolescent chubby cheeks. "Please let me stay. I don't have anywhere else to go." She looked at the last burger hungrily. "I haven't eaten in days."

"Have it," Cat said, nudging it towards her. "It's obvious you haven't been eating enough, your Bear looks like she's starving. Our forms are related more to nourishment, rather than our size as humans. What have you been doing, foraging?"

"Dumpster diving."

"Gross," Anita piped in, setting two slices of bread into the rusted toaster. "We'll feed you, at least." She gave Cat a withering glare. "I don't even know where we'd put you. The boys are already sharing, and I'm not about to share with a teenager."

"I can sleep in the living room! I promise I won't be a pain, and—"

"We should talk to the boys about this first," Cat said. "They live here, too."

"But what are we going to do with her?" Anita hissed, giving the toast a thick spread of butter and jelly. "We aren't her legal guardians, it's not like we can enroll her in the local high school."

"We'll worry about that when we get there. For now, let's just make sure she's fed and safe."

"Check her clothes from last night, make sure there aren't any trackers."

"I told you, I'm not a spy!" Delilah countered.

Cat's head was pounding. "Can you just humor my sister, please? She's clearly not going to let this go."

"Sure. I guess." Delilah crumpled the empty food packages. "Thanks for the food."

"Listen, kid, I know we're not the Bears you dreamed of, but we're going to try to do our best. You don't understand what it was like when we left the coast. We were totally on our own, for years. We didn't have anyone looking out for us."

Anita snorted. "Remember when we pulled that bait and switch at that gas station?"

"It was some true genius on your part," Cat said with a laugh, and then sobered. "I don't want to think about what would happen if we'd been caught."

"What was it like on the west coast?" Delilah asked.

"Our parents took us out there when we were young. We grew up in a Bear compound, it was kind of messy. Lots of angry Bears that never learned how to control themselves. Addiction. Lots of them running from the law after beating the hell out of some Normie at a bar."

"Oh," Delilah said quietly.

"We got some supplies together, we stole some money from the community fund, just enough to get us a bus ticket each, when the boys found out. We were so afraid they were going to rat us out, but they wanted to come with, even though they were underage. They didn't like the 'community,' either. Too much emphasis on isolation, on toeing the line and not asking any questions.

We didn't want to let them come with us, they were too young. We were worried enough they'd chase us down, much less if we took two Cubs with us."

Delilah bit the corner of a piece of toast. "So you left?"

"Yeah. The compound wasn't for us, but some are happy there, I guess. It's safer, in a lot of ways. Those Bears wouldn't be caught dead in a public park reserve."

"I'm sorry, I just... I didn't know where else to go. I don't know anything about being a Bear, not really."

"Our history isn't very well known outside compounds like the one we grew up in. It's secretive, protective." Cat sighed and closed her eyes. "You can stay, for now. But you'll need some new clothes. The boys are like string beans, their stuff is much too small."

"Catriona..." Anita said in a warning tone.

"I know. But if something had happened to me when we first left, I'd want some Bears to take you three in, to give you a chance. Even if it seemed shady as hell. I'll talk to the boys about something more permanent, but we're going to need some cash to keep her fed."

"We should keep our ears to the ground, then. Reach out to the Bears in Missouri, see if they've heard anything."

Cat shook her head. "I don't want anyone else to know about this. The Missouri Bears would want her down with them, and I'm not so sure that's best for her. This stays with us."

"This is risky as hell, Cat."

We'll just have to make sure we're as careful as we can be."

CHAPTER NINE

It had been three days since Andie heard from Cat, and even then, it had been a very cursory text, telling her that she was busy. Maybe she *had* misread something. Maybe Cat wasn't interested at all. She sipped on her coffee, sitting at the edge of her bed. She hadn't been back to Jazzy Java, either, ashamed to admit to Mara that her camera was irreparably broken, and thus she had nothing to barter for a bear claw with. Her stomach growled at the thought of the soft, fluffy, glazed pastry.

Nope. It was going to have to be bulk brand bran flakes, without milk, again. Outside, the sky was grey, and the air was crisp, frosting the corners of her poorly insulated window frames. It always felt strange in a season of such excess to be so painfully broke. She was glad she'd stocked up on Daisy's hay and food on her last paycheck. At least one of them was eating well.

Andie stabbed a spoon into the dry cereal and shoved it into her mouth. She'd been up half the night applying to any job she could find within a twenty-mile radius, from casual reception work, to working as a stocker at the local grocery store, to shift work as a line cook, which she definitely wasn't qualified for. Hours spent filling in her job history, only to be asked to attach her resume at the end. It was like a job in itself. There were no unemployment payments for the underemployed.

She sighed angrily and pushed the bowl away. She was sick of the taste, sick of struggling, and heartbroken over the loss of her camera, her one chance at becoming something that had a slightly better bottom line. Her phone stayed silent, but she checked it again. No messages. "No one loves me but you,

Daisy," she said to the sleeping chinchilla.

Her coffee was already cold. She set it on the table and flipped through an old photography magazine. Even thinking about it made her feel sick, though, so she shoved it into her nightstand and slammed the drawer shut. She opened her laptop, and it struggled to boot up, hanging on the loading screen for several minutes. Andie opened a notebook and sat it beside her, and began to apply for more shitty, dead-end jobs. The rent had to get paid somehow, no one else was going to do it for her, and not even her parents could help, being broke themselves after their car's transmission blew last month, followed by the boiler. She didn't want to worry them, so as far as they knew, she was doing just fine on her own.

Anything would be a welcome distraction from the endless stream of applications for jobs she'd never even get an interview for. A shop floor assistant job at the department store in the next town already had six hundred and thirty-two applicants. Strange how the news would boast of a growing economy, when people kept losing their jobs. Once the new development broke ground, it would breathe new life into the town, provide desperately needed jobs for people who were barely making rent. She clicked on a job listed fifteen miles away as a cleaner in an office building: three hundred and seventy-eight applicants. Snapping the laptop shut in frustration, she climbed off the bed and lingered by the fridge, wishing something good would magically appear within. She opened it and found the same crap as before. Half a bottle of ketchup, an onion that had started to sprout, and one beer leftover from her weekend with just her and Daisy. Too early to drink, not that one beer was even worth it.

A knock at the door startled her out of her hungry stupor. She padded to the door in her thick socks and yanked it open. "Sorry, I'm not interes—" she cut herself off. "Cat! What are you doing here?" She sounded too enthusiastic, even to herself.

"Finally managed to sneak out from under Anita's thumb," Cat answered with a grin.

"Are you feeling better?"

"Much."

"Did you want to..." Andie trailed off. "I mean, uh—"

"Oh God, I'm sorry, I should have called first. I just thought—"

"No, it's fine!"

Cat shifted her weight from foot to foot. "I just thought maybe, if you weren't busy, we could try for that date. If you want. If you're not busy. You're probably busy, aren't you?"

"No. Shockingly, there's not a lot of work for a photographer without a camera." She grimaced. "Not a lot of work, period."

"Well, I might know a place, if you want to go. If you still wanted to have that date, I mean."

"Yes!" Andie shouted, and then chewed the inside of her cheek. *Don't seem so eager, you loser*, she thought. "Uh, yeah, that could be fun. Let me just get my coat." She turned to grab her parka from the hook, feeling the silent blush creep up her neck and flood into her cheeks. "Where are we headed?"

"It's a surprise. But, uh, bring your boots."

"Sure thing." She shoved her feet into her warm winter boots she'd gotten half price at the thrift store last year, and snatched her scarf from the back of the door. "I'm ready."

"We'll have to take your car, I hope that's okay. Nita needed the truck."

Panic crawled up Andie's spine. Her car was a disgusting mess. "Can you just give me a minute? I have to, uh... I have to get some work stuff out of there."

"I'll help."

"No!" she shouted. "I mean, uh, it's fine, it will just be a minute. Wait here."

"What, are you hiding a dead body in the trunk, or something?"

"Maybe."

"Whatever it is, it's fine."

"Please just wait here?"

Cat furrowed her brow in concern. "Okay."

"Excellent. Meet me out front in like five minutes." Andie ran down the stairs and out the front door to her car, and started to pull the crap out of her car, mostly empty coffee cups from Jazzy Java and candy wrappers, and the garbage from her late night run for burgers the other night after leaving Cat's house. She'd been so hungry, she hadn't even made it home with them, scarfing them at red lights and stop signs instead. She tipped it all into the building's dumpster and unlocked the passenger side door for Cat, who was now waiting there for her.

"My truck gets messy too, you know."

"Probably not *that* messy."

"You'd be surprised."

Andie put the key into the ignition. "Right. Where to?"

"North on the highway."

"Hmm." Andie checked her gas gauge, which was hovering at a quarter of a tank.

"Don't worry, it's only about five miles out."

"Okay." She pulled the car into drive and pulled out of the parking space, weaving through the lot to miss all the potholes that management refused to fix. "Music?"

"I'd rather talk to you, if that's alright."

"Sure."

"I wanted to make sure you weren't too freaked out about the other night."

"No. I mean, yes, but no. I feel like... *Werebears*," she whispered, "might not even be the weirdest thing I ever see in my life."

"It's just, you didn't call, and..."

"I texted you! You said you were busy!"

Cat whipped out her phone. "What?" She scrolled and tapped, and sighed. "Anita. She must have replied while I was sleeping, and then deleted the evidence."

"Does your sister not like me, or something?"

"We just have a lot going on."

Andie turned onto the highway and accelerated to five miles under the speed limit. "That Bear?"

"Yeah. She's from out west. It's... complicated."

"We can talk about it, if you want."

"I've spent the past three days talking about it. I'm sick of talking about it."

She tugged on the seatbelt. "Follow those brown faded signs."

"For the old trail?"

"Yup."

"I thought that got closed down years ago."

"It did."

"Right." Andie settled in behind another car, waiting for her turnoff. It looked like it might snow. "So do you frequently trespass on old condemned trails, or is this a special treat?"

"I've never taken anyone here, actually. Not even my sister."

"Oh."

"It will be worth it, I promise."

"I trust you."

Cat smirked. "I mean, that much is obvious, you got into a car with a Bear and are driving to a secluded reserve."

"I didn't really think of that."

"It's okay, I already ate."

"Have you ever eaten a person?"

"*What?* No!"

Andie flipped on her turn signal. "I'm sorry, I just thought—"

"I tend to make sure I'm in a place where there's plenty of foraging. Stole some food from some careless campers once or twice. Ate a deer once, but the four of us shared it."

"I hear venison is nice."

"It is, especially when it's fresh. Always gives me indigestion after, though. I prefer to stick to berries and tubers during a shift, and eat some nice *cooked* meat after."

"If Weres are real, then what else is real?"

Cat shrugged. "Your guess is as good as mine. Some of us think that we evolved as a way to protect small community units from large predators. Others think we may have a completely different common ancestor, given the sterility that can occur when a Were has a kid with a..."

"A Normie?"

"Yeah."

"It all just feels so pretend, you know? Like, even though I saw it with my own eyes, I doubt myself."

"Trust me, it doesn't feel pretend to me," Cat said with a laugh. "When I'm trying to patch my jeans back together for the third or fourth time, it definitely feels real." She pointed off to the left. "The turn in is over there."

"Are we going to get into trouble for being here?"

"Maybe."

"What kind of trouble?"

"Relax, Andie. We're just two townies looking for a fun hike in the woods to get away from it all."

"Mm. Okay."

"What, are you afraid of that Ranger Dade?"

Andie pulled her car off the highway onto the tree-lined, cracked concrete road surface. It had been a long time since any maintenance had been done here. "I'm not afraid of Dade. I'm afraid of getting arrested. I have enough shit to be dealing with."

"We're not going to get arrested, alright? It's barely even trespassing, see? The trail head signs are still here, and there aren't chains to keep anyone out. Just trust me, alright?"

"Weren't you just lecturing me on how foolish it was to trust a Bear in the woods?"

"Theoretically. But I'm a *nice* Bear. And I promise not to eat you, scout's honor." She grimaced. "I don't think I could handle another off-cycle shift right now, anyway. I only just got rid of the last migraine."

"If it's scout's honor, then I guess I have no choice except to trust you."

"Exactly. Park over there, under the tree."

"Is it still a secret why we're here, or are you going to fill me in?" Andie asked, pulling the keys from the ignition.

"Still a secret. You have to follow me up the trail."

"I hope you know where you're going."

Cat climbed out of the car and slammed the door. "I have an excellent sense of direction, I'll have you know. I think it's from the Bear within. I've never gotten lost, not even once."

"Remind me to take you on my next road trip, then. My stupid GPS is always getting me turned around."

"I'd love that. Road trips are fun! Snacks, music, games in the car, weird, off the wall destinations like giant rocking chairs and salt and pepper shaker museums. Memories that last a lifetime."

"Sure, but we're sharing driving duties. I can't go longer than a few hours before my eyes start to cross."

"Come on, the trail is just over there," Cat said, running towards the mulched path that had long grown over with weeds and vines, now frosted with ice in the winter air. "It's not a long walk, maybe twenty minutes."

"Short date, then. You trying to welch on our deal?"

"Shut up," Cat said with a laugh. "It will be even shorter if we race to the trail fork."

"Please, you're a Bear, I bet you can run faster than anyone."

"Not when I'm like this."

"What do you get if you win?"

"I bet you didn't talk to Mara yet about that hot chocolate."

"I haven't been in there since my camera got smashed."

"Oh, Andie, I'm sorry," Cat said, and grabbed her gloved hand. "How much will it be for a replacement?"

"Too much. Five hundred at least."

"Jesus."

"Yeah. Anyway I don't really want to talk about it, I'm still trying to figure it out." Andie squeezed Cat's hand and closed her eyes, savoring the clean crispness of the air and the scent of pine drifting around them. "You're on."

"What?"

"You're on!" Andie released Cat's hand and tore off down the trail, dodging low-hanging tree branches and swerving around dried up thorned vines that snagged at her coat. Cat's footsteps echoed close behind her, racing to catch up.

"Cheater!" Cat shouted after her, laughing.

"I need a head start against someone like you!"

"You don't even know where you're going!"

Andie ducked under a pine bough. "I'm sure I'll figure it out!"

"Left! Go left!"

She turned back to see where Cat was, and smacked right into a felled tree, falling over the other side. "And you call *me* a cheater! You led me right into a trap!"

"It's not a trap if you pay attention to what's in front of you," Cat said, climbing over the tree, breathless. "Look."

The trail had led them down into a rocky canyon, with a sparkling waterfall that fell into a pool of water, with red leaves from the trees above gently rippling the surface when they landed. "Holy shit," Andie breathed. "How did I not know this was here?"

"Not many do. The county pushes people to the reserve. It's bigger, better signposted, more facilities. This place is smaller. No room for Bears, not really. Nowhere to run if we got cornered. Bad at climbing."

The quiet roar of the water immediately soothed Andie's nerves and made her feel totally at peace, like there was some ancient magic hiding underneath the damp earth. "How often do you come here?"

Cat shrugged. "Once in a while, I guess. The others don't really like it here."

"*Why?*"

"Not outdoorsy."

"But... they're *Bears.*"

"We only have paws a few nights out of the month. Besides, if Bears could do their shifts in a five star hotel, Anita would be all over that. She is not the kind of girl who enjoys nature. She'd rather live in a city, but... well, that's risky."

"This is beautiful."

"I'm glad you like it," Cat said, putting her hand in hers again.

"I can't help but think of all the photos I would take if I had my camera here, even though I'm not much of a landscape photographer. Long shutter, filters, pump up certain color profiles in post. It would look magical, like somewhere a fairy would live." She furrowed her brow. "There aren't fairies, are there?"

"Your guess is as good as mine."

"Thank you for bringing me here."

"So what did you want to claim as a prize?"

"What?"

Cat moved closer. "I mean, since you won the race and all, even if you did trip over the finish line."

"Oh." Andie's heart raced faster than it had when she was faced with poachers and Bears, looking down into Cat's pretty brown eyes. "I, uh... I dunno." She could practically feel her brain misfiring, giving her all the wrong things to say. She kept her mouth shut.

"Are you okay?"

"It's snowing." Fat, fluffy white blobs had begun to fall from the heavy sky, and were already starting to settle on the mossy rocks near the water. Their clouds of breath mingled together in the air, intertwining, before spiraling up through the canyon, and dissipating into the falling snow.

"This is nice," Cat said, grasping the extra fabric of Andie's coat and pulling her closer. "It's so quiet."

Blood pounded in Andie's ears. How the hell was this scarier than looking down the muzzle of a rifle? "It's always quiet at my apartment," she said, finally. "Just me and Daisy."

"Who the hell is Daisy?"

"My chinchilla."

Cat laughed. "Right."

"I'm a one-woman... woman," Andie said. "Or maybe more accurately, a one-Bear woman?"

"You're rambling."

"I'm nervous."

"Of what? Me?"

"Of this." Andie gathered every ounce of courage within her, and pulled Cat's face to hers, kissing her gently on her soft lips. She felt like there were explosions in her brain, like she wanted to scream, and laugh, and cry, all at the same time.

Cat kissed her back, wrapping her arms around Andie's neck and leaning into her, the soft sighs from their warm mouths despite the icy air melding seamlessly with the bubbled rush of water from the falls. Had anything in the world ever been so perfect, so right? No. Never.

"Cat," she whispered, pressing their cold noses together.

"Yeah?"

"I never want to leave this place."

"Me neither."

They kissed again, and Andie wrapped her tight in her arms, settling around Cat's waist. Snow was falling thick and fast now, and she resented that the worry about her car's tires interrupted the moment. If only they could stay in that moment forever, and never have to deal with rent, or park rangers, or Bears from far away, or broken cameras. With Cat in her arms, she almost felt invincible.

"The snow is sticking," Andie said softly.

"I guess we should go."

"Should I take you home?"

"No." Cat nuzzled Andie's neck. "Let's make dinner together. I want to see your apartment for real, I want to spend more time with you. I don't want to go home."

"What about the new Bear?"

"Delilah will be fine with the others for a night. The boys are only too eager to teach her how to be a Bear. It's like she's the little sister they never had."

"I don't have any food at home, unless you want dry cereal or ramen noodles."

"Stop by the store, I got paid today. I can treat us to some spaghetti, a jar of sauce, and a bottle of two-buck-chuck."

Andie pulled her into a kiss again. "I wish we could stay."

"We can come back soon, once the roads are cleared. Tomorrow, or the next day."

"You haven't had enough of me yet?"

"Nope." Cat snuggled into her and sighed. "And you're not getting rid of me that easy."

CHAPTER TEN

When Andie pushed open the door to her apartment, Cat eagerly shuffled inside. The canyon was beautiful, but it was damn cold outside, and the snow was already two inches deep on some of the side roads. It would be hell trying to get home later. "Cute place," she said, and meant it. It was small, but welcoming.

"I don't have a couch, you'll have to sit on the bed or on the stools at the table."

"You making me dinner?"

"You paid, I'll cook," Andie said, unloading the tote bags onto the small counter. "I think I can manage it."

"Pour us a glass of that cheap ass wine, I'm freezing."

Andie nodded, pouring wine into two mugs. "I would have thought Bears didn't get cold."

"I don't have my fur at the moment, yes, it's fucking cold," Cat said with a laugh, pulling her coat tight around her. "And this must be Daisy?" she asked, approaching the generously sized cage. The little beast inside, with huge ears and a dense fluffy coat started to shout, or bark, whatever it was, and Cat nearly tripped over herself trying to back away. "Shit, I don't think she likes me."

"She's just timid," Andie said, rushing to the cage to comfort her.

"No, some animals don't like Bears. It's like they can sense it."

"Hmm. Maybe she'll warm up to you. We can try, if you want."

"I don't want to scare her."

Andie went back into the small kitchen and returned with a small box of raisins. "You can usually bribe Daisy. She *loves* treats. Just don't give her too many, she's a little greedling."

"Aren't we all?"

"Sit on the floor with your legs out in front of you. I'll set her down, and you can offer her a raisin."

"Okay." Cat sat down and took the box of raisins. "Will she bite?"

"Is a Bear really scared of a chinchilla?"

"Tiny teeth still hurt."

"She's pretty gentle, I don't think she will bite unless you grab her."

Cat shook her head. "I wouldn't do that."

"Here we go," Andie said, setting Daisy on the floor. "Get some treats, Dais!"

"Who doesn't want some dessert, right?" Cat asked, setting a raisin on the floor near her. "I'm just a big teddy bear, I won't hurt you."

Daisy approached cautiously, zig-zagging across the floor, sniffing the air. She snatched the treat and ran back to the safety of Andie's shadow.

"Rip the next one in half and put it a little closer."

"Come on, Daisy," Cat cooed. She really was a cute little thing, like a giant, cuddly mouse. The chinchilla came back, closer this time, and stayed while she munched on the treat.

"One more, on your lap this time," Andie whispered. "Unzip your jacket."

"See, I'm not dangerous, am I?" This time, Daisy climbed into Cat's lap and chewed the last bit of raisin. "Oh my God, she's so cute."

"She likes to snuggle in your shirt, if you hold her in there like a little hammock."

"Can I?"

"Sure."

Cat folded up the edge of her shirt and rocked gently until Daisy curled up, making tiny little squeaking sounds. "Hey, it worked."

"I told you she was easily bribed."

"I bet she's good company."

Andie went back into the kitchen to stir the pot of sauce. "She is, when she's not sleeping. Daisy gets grumpy if I wake her up."

"Well, I'd be grumpy too, if someone woke me up," Cat said to the little creature nestled in her shirt.

"She's going to love you forever, now that you gave her treats. Raisins are her favorite, or dried cranberries." Andie set some leafy vegetables into the cage along with some fresh hay. "She'd eat the whole box if I let her, but she needs her veggies, too."

Cat's stomach growled. "When's dinner?"

"In a minute, I just have to drain it. You can set her back in her cage when you're done bonding."

"Can I play with her again sometime?"

"Of course! I didn't think you'd like her, I thought you'd prefer something... more dangerous."

"Andie, there's something you should know about me."

"I already know you're a WereBear."

"Well yes, that, but also, I'm incredibly risk-averse. A chinchilla is exactly my speed, I think."

Andie snorted. "Imagine, a Bear being risk-averse."

"In my defense, actual bears are, too. We all just want to be left alone, really, to eat some fish and berries and wander around in the forest."

"Sounds like the perfect life to me."

"Yeah," Cat agreed, setting Daisy back into her cage, "it's not bad. Being broke as hell sure sucks, though. Hard to hold a salaried job when you get sick after a non-cycle shift, or spend all your time worried the park ranger is going to show up and cramp your style."

"What would you be, if you could do anything?"

"A nurse."

Andie set the plates on the table. "I see that. You're very gentle and caring."

"Oh," Cat replied, blushing. "That's very nice of you to say."

"It's the truth."

"I went all the way through school, you know. Aced every test. Couldn't get through the practical because they were so inflexible on timing, and I just couldn't get around it with shifts."

"That's terrible."

Cat slid onto the wobbly stool. "I tried loads of different hospitals and programs, none would accept me if I said I was unavailable at certain times of the month. Seeing as I can't exactly disclose why, well... it just didn't work out for me." She twirled her fork around some spaghetti, eager to change the topic. "You know, some house plants would really liven this place up."

"I have what some people would call a black thumb. I can't keep anything alive, not even the stuff people swear is immortal." Andie looked at her over her mug of wine. "You're not immortal, are you?"

"No."

"Anyway, I've tried having plants in here, they all croak after a week or two."

"What about some lettuce for Daisy?"

"I wouldn't want to disappoint her with my inability to keep it alive long enough to have some leaves to harvest."

"Hmm. We'll see about that."

Andie laughed. "What are you going to do, sneak in when I'm not here and leave plants on the windowsills?"

"Maybe."

"Well, then you'd better be ready to sneak back in to water them, too, or all your effort will be for nothing."

"Spaghetti is good."

"Yeah, it's alright, I guess it's good I managed to cook something without burning the water." Andie slurped up a forkful of pasta. "Thank you for dinner."

"Thank you for the date." Cat sipped the wine, which almost didn't taste like diesel. "I wish it didn't have to end."

"Looking at that snow outside, it's going to be a hell of a time getting you home. I bet the taxis aren't even running right now, and I don't trust my car in the snow." She raised her mug. "Not to mention, I've been drinking."

"I don't want to ask my sister or the boys to come get me, not before the roads get plowed and salted." It wasn't untrue, but really, she just wasn't ready to go home yet. She wanted to stay with Andie in her cozy, quiet apartment, and feel safe for just a little while longer.

"You could always..." Andie trailed off.

"Stay?" Cat asked hopefully.

"I don't want to be presumptuous."

"It's for safety."

Andie grinned. "Yeah. It's the responsible thing to do. More wine?"

"Yes, please."

As Andie topped up Cat's wine glass, she scooted her stool closer to hers. "You should put some lights up or something in here. Get a little bit festive."

"I haven't really been feeling it, this year."

"What if I said that was important to me?"

"Then I'd do it."

"Really?"

"Yeah."

Cat interlaced her fingers with Andie's. "Maybe date number two can be hunting down the scrawniest, saddest Christmas tree we can find."

"Why the scrawniest?" Andie asked with a laugh.

"I feel sorry for them. It's not their fault no one wants them. Besides, they're cheap. Have you seen what they're charging for trees these days?"

"To be honest, I don't usually bother with them. It's just me and Daisy every year. She gets extra raisins, I get a microwave turkey dinner and a slice of frozen pie from the store."

"That's..." It might have been one of the saddest things she'd ever heard. Holidays with her sister and the boys were never fancy, but at least they had each other. "That sounds lonely," Cat finished.

Andie scraped the last of the spaghetti from her bowl. "Yeah."

"Maybe you could spend this year with us. If you wanted, it's—"

"You should probably ask your Bear family about that first."

"Oh." Cat drained her mug. "Yeah. I guess you're right."

"I'll wash up, you can find something on television if you want."

"Sure." Cat climbed up on the bed, wrapping herself in the soft, worn throw that was draped over the corner. She flicked through the stations, flipping past the nightly news, a celebrity reality show, and a game show, settling on an old Christmas movie she used to watch when she was a kid. "Is this okay?"

Andie poked her head out of the kitchen. "Oh, I love this one. Turn it up."

"Hurry, it's about to start." The sweeping orchestral intro burst through the tiny box television's tinny speakers just as Andie crawled into the bed behind her and wrapped her arms around her.

"Are you warm enough?"

"I am now." She texted her sister not to worry, and tossed her phone to the other side. "This is nice."

"Definitely the best night I've had all year," Andie replied, kissing her gently on the neck. "I wish it could always be like this." She pulled back and drew her knees up to her chest. "Sorry, I just mean—"

"It's fine," Cat soothed, kissing her softly, and running her hands over the outside of Andie's hoodie. "I know exactly what you mean." She crawled beneath the covers and patted the bed. "Now come on, let's watch this."

Cat was already falling asleep fifteen minutes in. She must have been more tired than she thought.

CHAPTER ELEVEN

Andie was leaving the real estate development office, breathing a sigh of relief. With the new building all squared away, she'd be getting ten more hours a week, enough to catch up on her bills in a few months, and start saving for a new camera. It was the good news she'd been waiting for, and after scraping through her bag for spare change to put gas in her car again, she was looking forward to not being quite so flat broke in the near future. Maybe she'd even be able to put some money away for a cheap weekend trip away with Cat, once the weather started getting warmer in the spring.

The mid-morning sky was bright and clear, though still cold enough to keep the snow from melting in the muddy banks on the sides of the road where the plows pushed it. She breathed in the clean, crisp air, and heaved a sigh of relief. Maybe things would turn out alright, after all. The new building would break ground in a week, and as soon as construction commenced, it would be her job to get photo evidence of the progress for the investors. The photos the reception staff had been taking were blurry and incorrectly framed.

She paused to rifle through her messenger bag, looking for her phone to text Cat the good news. The gentle night they'd spent together had been just what Andie needed to break out of her funk. The deadline for the wildlife competition was the same day as the new building breaking ground, and her camera was still toast, but she'd just try again next year. It made a world of difference to have at least one thing going right in her life.

"Andie?"

She looked up and met the stunned faces of Cat and her sister, Anita. "Hey!

I was just going to text you."

"What are you doing here?"

Andie tilted her head quizzically. "What do you mean what am I doing here? I work here. What are *you* doing here?"

"We're handing in a petition to block the new building," Anita said flatly, holding out a clipboard filled with signatures. "You work for these assholes?"

"I thought you knew that."

"No, I didn't *know that*!" Cat said through gritted teeth, her voice raising in volume. "Don't you know what they're trying to do to the reserve?"

"The new building will bring in lots of jobs—"

"Are you stupid?" Anita barked, laughing. "These Syndicorp assholes are going to be busing people in and out, there's not going to be any jobs."

"Well they gave me one," Andie said defiantly, feeling a hot anger creep across her chest. "And it's going to pay the bills I wasn't going to be able to without my camera."

"Fucking photographers," Anita scoffed, nudging her sister. "I'm glad you broke it."

"Shut up," Cat said, narrowing her eyes at her sister.

"What? I thought you said—"

"Shut. Up. Anita."

Andie glared from one sister to the other, the truth dawning. "I thought you said you didn't have any control when you were shifted."

"That's—it's not exactly true. But what I can't believe is that you willingly shill for these monsters!"

"No. No, hang on here. You broke my camera on purpose?" It was like she could feel her heart breaking in real time.

"It's not like I had a choice, I—"

"Of course you had a choice!" Andie shouted, her eyes filling with tears. "You could have trusted me!"

"I don't *know* you!"

"Will you two keep it down?" Anita hissed. "We don't need the entire town knowing our business, yeah?"

"Don't worry, I'm going," Andie spat. "We're done."

"We weren't even anything to begin with!" Cat shot back. "I wouldn't have even bothered with you in the first place if I knew you had zero morals!"

Andie was already stalking back to her car. "Whatever."

"How could you betray us?"

"Bills have to get paid, Cat," Andie said, wrenching open the door to her car, wiping away the angry tears that were already darkening the collar of her coat. "I thought you of all people would understand that."

* * *

Andie sat in her car, parked in a sparse parking lot behind the grocery store, next to the street lamp that hadn't worked for at least five years. She dialed her friend Mercy's phone number. It went straight to voicemail. She dialed Parker's number, and he picked up.

"Hello darling!" he chimed. "I haven't heard from you in ages!"

"I texted you twice last week, you never responded."

"Well it's been absolutely crazy at work up here, you know how it is, in fact I'm about to go into a meeting right now, and—" someone who sounded exactly like Mercy laughed in the background. "Oh, don't! You know I can't with that, not with all the work at the paper I have to do."

"Are you—are you both out to dinner? Without me?"

"Well, we know you've been struggling lately, we didn't want to make you feel bad."

"I could have just had a coffee or something, I miss you guys."

"Andie... I'm sorry, love, I am, and Mercy is sorry too. We'll get together soon, we promise. Anyway, our food's here so..."

"Bye."

"Talk soon."

Andie leaned back into the headrest, trying to stem the tide of angry, silent tears that continued to slide down her face. She dialed her mom's number and hesitated over the green send button. Was it really worth it to worry them over something so trivial? Cat was right, they *didn't* know each other. Maybe it was just a fling, or a very weird fever dream. She erased the numbers one by one, and set her phone on the passenger's seat.

The sun was already starting to set, emblazoning the tips of the tallest pine trees on the horizon with its winter fire. If she hadn't gotten banned from the reserve, she'd go for a hike before it got dark. Maybe Cat had sold her out to the ranger, too, making sure she wouldn't come back. Andie felt her jaw clench every time she thought about Cat, and yet, when her phone began to ring, vibrating against the worn fabric of the seat, Andie still hoped it was her.

"Hello?"

"Andrea!"

"Mom?"

"I was thinking of you and thought I'd call."

"That's weird, I was about to call you."

"How are you?"

Andie took a deep breath. "Okay."

"How are you, *really*?"

"Oh, you know," she said with a sigh. "Same old."

"Dad got a new job working up at the school. Head janitor."

"That's great! Tell him I said I'm proud."

"Honey?" Her mother said, her voice muffled like she was covering the phone with her hand. "Andrea says she's proud of you." She laughed, and the sound was clear again. "He says thank you."

"How is everything up there?" Andie asked, poking through her glove box absentmindedly. "Other than the new job."

"Keeping busy, as always, you know." There was a long pause. "We worry about you, you know. Across the country all by yourself, especially this time of year."

"I'm fine, Mom."

"Are you seeing anyone special?"

Andie rankled. "No."

"Who is she?"

"It doesn't matter, it's stopped dead in its tracks."

"Hmm. Well how's work?"

"Fine, I guess."

"Did you enter that competition you were talking about over the summer?"

"No." Andie's fingers fell on a receipt from months back, when she bought a lens for her camera. She frowned. "I decided to try next year, instead."

"That's not like you. Are you sure there's nothing wrong?"

"Yes," she spat, and then immediately regretted it. "I'm sorry, Mom. I'm just a little distracted."

"You know, Andrea, love isn't always easy. Sometimes you have to work for it."

"Who said anything about love?"

"No one. But a mother always knows, and I can hear the heartbreak in your voice." Her mother sighed. "You don't have to tell me what happened, and I suspect you won't, not if you're this upset. All I'll say is that walking that mile in someone else's shoes can clear up a lot of anger and hurt."

"You're probably right." Andie flipped the receipt over in her hands. "But it's her who needs to do the walking."

"Alright well, I guess I'll let you go. Sounds like you have plenty to be thinking about."

"Thanks for checking in, Mom."

"As long as you're sure you're alright. And you're probably not planning on it, but don't worry about coming back for Christmas, I've gotta work and your Dad is on call. He didn't want to be requesting time off right out of the gate, you know."

"Yeah." It was like this every year, and this one would be no different. Work, cars breaking down, money, there was always a reason, and given how contentious things had been when Andie was a kid, she wasn't in any hurry. One phone call every few months was plenty.

"Okay. Love you, Andrea."

"Love you too, Mom." She hung up the phone, examining the receipt paper in her hands. It gave her an idea. It was one hell of a long shot, but she had to try. It was the only way she could get out of this mess.

CHAPTER TWELVE

Anita knocked on the door to Cat's room, and eased it open. "You still mad?"

"Yeah, I'm still mad. You shouldn't have said anything."

"She's working for *them*!"

"Yeah, and maybe we could have had a conversation about it, but now she knows I intentionally stomped on and crushed her camera."

"You did it to keep us all safe."

Cat picked a piece of lint off her bear pajamas. "That doesn't mean it was the right thing to do."

"It was for us."

"I don't want to talk about it. Just leave me alone, Nita."

"I made dinner."

"I'm not hungry."

"That's bullshit," Anita said, perching at the edge of the bed. "You're always hungry."

"I've lost my appetite."

"I said I was sorry, Catriona!"

"And I said, I don't want to talk about it!"

"Well how was I supposed to know?"

Cat turned and faced the wall to hide the tears gathering in her eyes. "Use your head, Sis. Why the hell would I have told Andie I smashed her camera on purpose? Jesus, those things are like five hundred dollars. Double that, even!"

"You had to, though. If she'd sold on that footage—"

"She wouldn't have."

"You didn't know that then."

"I should have." Cat sighed and wiped the tears from her cheeks. "Who would believe it was real, anyway? People would probably just think it was a hoax by an effects studio to get attention from big budget projects. I bet no one even would have cared." She ran a hand through her hair. "But Andie's a good person. She's just trying to get by, like the rest of us—"

"The rest of us manage without working for Syndicorp," Anita interrupted.

"She wouldn't have sold the footage. She was right, I should have trusted her."

"We've spent our entire adult lives running from something. We've had it beat into our brains to keep what we are secret, and safe. You were just acting on instincts that were burned into you a long time ago."

"I have to make it right, Nita."

"Well, what are you going to do? It's not like we have five hundred big ones lying around to just get her a new one."

"I don't know. I need to research."

"You know I love you, right?"

"Yeah. And you know I'd do anything for you, despite your big mouth and refusal to apologize in a genuine way because you are even more stubborn than I am."

Anita reached out and put a hand on her shoulder. "I am sorry, Cat. Really."

"You're forgiven. Mostly. But you still have to help me fix it."

"And how are we going to fit that in, around fighting the county's desperation to bulldoze half the reserve and worrying about a teenaged Bear runaway?"

"I guess we should start with some food."

* * *

Cat couldn't sleep. She tossed and turned, unable to turn off the scenes replaying over and over in her mind. Leaving the compound with Anita and the boys. The years of running and close shaves. Getting letter after letter in the mail with job rejections, saying she'd never be a nurse if she had to take so much time off. Smashing Andie's camera. She sighed angrily and threw off the covers, shoving her feet into her slippers.

The house was quiet, and the kitchen dark. The others were sleeping, and it was hours until sunrise, but her stomach growled insistently. Getting hungry in the middle of the night wasn't the most unusual thing to ever happen, but it was more annoying when there wasn't much nice stuff around to eat. This time of year, their appetites increased, despite not actually going into hibernation. They'd start sleeping more, and if they didn't get enough, they'd get sick, miss work.

She opened the refrigerator and frowned at the emptiness. Someone's leftovers from dinner, covered in foil, and not much else. The pantry wasn't as well stocked as she'd like, either - some cans of alphabet soup, three packs of instant noodles, and a third of a pack of rice. Not much to work with. They'd have to find money somewhere to go grocery shopping, especially with Delilah staying with them now.

The kitchen light flicked on, revealing Luke and Felix in the doorway. "Hey," Luke said, sitting at the table. "Couldn't sleep?"

"No. You either?"

Felix shook his head. "Too much on our minds. Either that, or Luke is snoring too loud. Hard to tell." His big, mischievous brown eyes twinkled.

"Oh please," Luke said, shoving him playfully. "As if you aren't like, the loudest Bear ever."

"Whatever, man. Your snoring could wake the dead."

Cat nodded. "It's true. Sometimes I hear you in *my* room."

"Check the freezer," Felix said, a grin spreading across his face. "We might find a nice midnight snack in there."

"Oh really?"

"Something I brought home from my apprenticeship today."

"How's that going, anyway?" Cat asked, pulling at the freezer door. There was a mysterious box inside.

Felix nodded. "Good. In a few weeks they'll start letting me help out on the big catering jobs. They'll need the extra help for holiday parties and stuff."

"So what is it?"

"Open it!"

She set the box on the counter and pried up a corner with her fingernail. "Whoa, is this chicken parmesan?"

"Yeah. There's enough for all of us, if we share."

"What about Anita and Delilah?"

Felix shrugged. "We can save them some, I guess. Put it in the microwave. Actually, no, I'll do it. I bet you'll have it on too high and dry it out."

"Oh ho ho, master chef," Cat said with a laugh. "You're already putting my mediocre cooking skills to complete shame."

"It's not like it takes much," he said, emptying the box onto a plate and putting it in the microwave. "You manage to burn water."

"That was *one* time." Cat sat back down and rubbed her eyes. "How about you, Luke? How are things?"

"Yeah, good. Learned some drywall today." He looked down at the floor. "I was thinking maybe eventually I might try to go to school to be an architect."

"You should!" she shouted excitedly. "How cool would *that* be?"

"It's a ways off, don't scream the house down and wake everyone up," Luke said nonchalantly. "It's just something I'm considering."

"Well, whatever you decide, we'll make it happen one way or another, okay? I mean, hell, apparently with Felix's job we'll be eating like royalty."

"Don't expect this every night," Felix said, depositing the plate and several forks onto the table. "But I'll do my best when there're extras."

The chicken was moist and succulent, the cheese stringy and delicious. It was the best meal she'd had since the pasta at Andie's. Her heart ached at the thought. "I don't know if there's going to be any left when we get through with it," she said, diving in with her fork for another bite.

"The hell you say," Anita said, snatching the fork from her hand as she leaped into the kitchen, looking like she, too, hadn't slept. She shoved the bite in her mouth, laughing.

"Bitch," Cat griped, taking the fork back. "You could have just asked."

"Scoot over, I want some," Anita said, perching on the arm of Cat's chair. "You could at least tell a Bear when you're foraging at midnight."

"We thought you were sleeping!"

"Yeah, right. This is so good, I can't even blame you for trying to hold out on me."

Luke blocked Felix from taking another bite. "Maybe we should wake up Delilah, she might want some."

"I'm already awake," a small voice said from the other room. "I just didn't want to be rude." She appeared in the doorway in her mismatched, ill-fitting pajamas.

"Did we wake you up?" Cat asked.

"No, I couldn't sleep." She eyed the plate curiously. "Can I have some?"

"Here, take the rest of mine," Luke said, giving up his seat.

Cat gave her fork back to Anita. "We're going to have to figure out how to get you back in school. If someone from the foster system finds you here, we could get into trouble."

"I don't want anyone to get in trouble because of me. Maybe... maybe if it comes to that, I should just go back with them. Though I'm not sure my foster parents want anything to do with me anymore."

"They'll take you back to those people over my dead, grizzled body," Cat growled. "You're not going anywhere."

Luke stepped up behind Delilah and laid a protective, brotherly hand on her shoulder. "You're with us now. You're family."

CHAPTER THIRTEEN

Andie swung open the door to her apartment building, triumphant. She couldn't believe that she managed to pull that off. It was the first good news in days, since Cat all but told her to go and screw herself. Despite her anger, she kept checking her phone, only to be disappointed to find an empty screen. Climbing the steps to her apartment, she enjoyed the feeling of her camera bag over her shoulder again. The week without it had been devoid of any energy or excitement... except for the date with Cat. That had been magical.

She shook her head. No. No more of that. Distracted, she nearly tripped over the cloth tote bag sitting on her faded welcome mat. No one was around who could have left it, the hallways were quiet. Had it been left by a neighbor? Andie slid her key into the lock and pushed into her apartment, nudging the bag in with the toe of her boot. She hoped it was Christmas cookies from the apartment upstairs; last year the teen boy who lived there made the most beautiful macarons she'd ever seen, perfectly round and pink, lined up in orderly little rows.

Holding the borrowed camera in her hands, her creativity and enthusiasm surged through her fingertips. Finally, she was feeling like herself again. The woman behind the lens. She peered through the viewfinder, pointing the camera at Daisy's cage. "Daisy!" she called. "Look at me, sweetpea!"

Daisy rolled over and went back to sleep.

"I bet you'd pose if I had a box of treats," Andie muttered. But a photo of a chinchilla wasn't going to win a wildlife photography competition, especially not a lazy one in a cage. "I also bet as soon as I pull your dinner out, you're going to get very excited."

She rummaged through the fridge, frowning. "Not much left dinner left in here, Dais." The chinchilla stirred, giving little squeaks. "Oh, sure, *that* you understand." The last of the lettuce leaves were for Daisy, not that Andie really wanted a salad, anyway. She set them in the cage and gave the chinchilla gentle pets on the head. "Don't think you're getting out of movie night, either."

The bag was still sitting by the door. Andie grabbed the handles and peered inside, almost able to taste the cookies. "The hell?" she muttered to herself. Dropping the bag to the floor, she removed two long, flat trays of dirt, along with a note.

"Water when the soil is dry to the touch. Place in north-facing window. Lettuce seeds for Daisy.

-Cat

PS: I'm sorry."

If this was her idea of an apology, it sucked. A thoughtful gift of lettuce plants wasn't going to undo the fact that Cat had destroyed Andie's camera on purpose. An accident was one thing, especially in the midst of chaos, but for her to intentionally smash it? To Andie, that was almost unforgivable. It was her career, her life. It's not like it was a carton of spilled milk she was upset about. She zipped the camera back into the padded bag and flipped her phone around in her hands.

Was she being too stubborn? After all, this was obviously an olive branch from Cat, an attempt to make peace after their terrible argument. Andie poked the damp soil. It was a cute gift. Daisy would get some use out of it, if Andie managed to keep the plants alive long enough to harvest some leaves.

Of course Cat smashed the camera. She has to protect the other Bears, Andie understood that. But to lie about it? To not say anything, even after the fact, before their date? Andie scowled. What the hell was Cat's game, anyway? She wasn't sure if she felt more used or heartbroken. Lettuce seeds. It was laughable.

Yet, part of her wanted to text Cat immediately, to invite her over, to kiss her soft, warm lips and hold her in her arms. Her hand hovered over her phone. No. Her emotions were still too jumbled for this. It was too... complicated.

Daisy munched noisily on the leaves, scrabbling in her cage. For her own dinner, Andie made some instant noodles, again, the savory chicken flavor like ash in her mouth. Not even the last of the hot sauce could save the taste. Someday, she'd be able to buy her groceries without having to add each item to the calculator in her head, doing her best to account for the tax that would be added at checkout. She shoveled another forkful in, trying not to taste it. The spaghetti she'd shared with Cat was long gone, and so was the potential for their budding relationship.

* * *

"Andie!" Mara shouted excitedly, waving from behind the counter, now festooned with a wreath of fake holly and accompanying plastic pine boughs strung from one end to the other. The cafe was warm and inviting, the yellow-tinged lights glowing in the window. Even the bells on the door sounded more festive, despite their sameness.

"Hey."

"I feel like it's been forever since I've seen you in here!"

Andie scrunched up her face. "It's been, like, a week."

"Well, maybe we miss seeing you around here."

"My camera got smashed, so..."

"You don't think we only like having you here because you take pictures for our social media, do you?" Mara asked, bemused. "Andie, I like you because you're my friend."

"Oh. I guess I didn't think you thought of me as a friend."

"You're more than just your job, you know."

"Hmm." Andie unzipped her camera bag. "We should get some photos of the decorations, I bet people will love that. Here, stand behind the counter like you're about to serve someone. Perfect." The shutter of the borrowed camera swished closed several times before she stood back, scrolling through the gallery and admiring her work. "Not bad."

"So if your camera got wrecked, what's that around your neck?"

"Rental. Kind of."

"Sit on the stool here, I'll fix you something."

"No, no, I'm fine—"

Mara took one of the large ceramic mugs from a hook. "Shh. I'd say it's on the house, but someone already pre-paid for the next time you came in."

"Who?"

"I was told you'd know who it was from."

Cat, thought Andie.

"I was also told you might like one of these," Mara said, pushing a bear claw on a plate across the bar.

"Well, I'm not going to turn down my favorite food, am I?" It was still a hollow gesture, but at least this time it was something Andie could eat.

"Coffee?"

"Tea, if you have it. Green."

"You know we do!" Mara poured steaming hot water into the mug, releasing the scent of lemon and honey along with the earthy green tea. "So tell me about this kind of rental camera. Did it fall off the back of a truck?"

Andie laughed. "No. It's from the camera shop a few towns over. You know it?"

"Yeah, in the strip mall next to the movie theater."

"That's the one. Well, after a week without my camera, I was starting to get a little desperate. I drove up there a couple days ago, to see if they'd consider renting one out to me, even though they don't really have a program like that."

"And it worked!"

"Well, kind of," Andie grimaced. "I had to agree to teach their intro to digital photography class for teens on Saturdays."

"Only you could walk in somewhere as a customer, and leave an employee."

"I'm not going to be working there, it's too small a place. But it's lucky I've spent the past decade going there instead of the big chain place in Bloomingvale, at least they knew I wasn't lying." She sighed and blew on her piping hot tea. "At least I've got a camera back in my hands," she continued, "if for no other reason than I get to take pictures for Jazzy Java."

Mara snorted. "Please. Some day you'll be some big shot photographer, you won't have time for us anymore. You'll be off taking pictures of rare animals in the restricted areas of national parks, thinking about how boring your life was when you traded photos for coffee here."

"I'd never call Jazzy Java boring!"

"We'll see. So tell me about this class you'll be teaching. How many kids? Will you get paid?"

"It's not paid. It's a community outreach thing, to get kids from the community to come learn to take pictures for free. They asked me to do it in exchange for the rental camera."

"Professor Andie Zanetti. It has a ring to it."

"I'm no professor. I'm just glad it worked out. It feels like it's a one-in-a-million thing."

"Speaking of which..." Mara trailed off.

"No."

"I'm just saying, she seems into you. And she's cute!"

"Yeah she's probably like, the most beautiful woman I've ever seen, but it's not going to work."

"What? Why?"

"She doesn't like that I work for that real estate development company."

Mara frowned. "The one that won the bid to build that new place over by the reserve?"

"Yeah."

"Listen, Andie, I wasn't going to say anything, but..."

"But what?"

"You know that company has big ties with Syndicorp, right?"

"Well sure, I assumed, given they won the bid. I think I heard that they did some work together before, out in Tucson or something."

"Syndicorp owns a majority stake in that development company."

"Oh."

"And that development company owns this building. Andie, we got a letter four days ago that our rent is going up two hundred percent."

"What? They can't do that!"

Mara shrugged. "They said what we've been paying 'isn't in line with the current market rate,'" she said, making air quotes with her fingers, her nails painted red with white snowflakes for the season. "It was baked into our initial contract, but we never thought they'd raise it that much all at once."

"Bastards."

"If we can't argue them back down to something reasonable, I don't know if we'll be able to stay open. We were only just starting to make a little bit of profit, you know?"

"Is there anything I can do?" Andie asked.

"We're thinking of starting a petition, but I don't know how much good that will do. What are your contacts like over there? Do you know anyone who might be able to help?"

"I don't know many people, but I can definitely try. You've worked too hard on this place for them to close your doors like that. Haven't they noticed all the empty places around here? Market rate, my ass, Applefield is hardly some bustling metropolis."

"Do you think you could talk to them tomorrow?"

"Of course I will. I have to meet someone at the office anyway, to let me into one of the properties that doesn't have a lock box with the key. I'll ask them what exactly they are thinking, what a totally bone-headed idea to raise your rent. Who's going to be in here, if not for you?"

Mara wiped the bar with a clean rag, scrubbing at a small sticky patch where a coffee syrup had dripped. "Probably a big chain, if our new landlords are to be believed."

"With all those burnt coffee grounds?" Andie made a face and stuck out her tongue. "No, thanks." She bit into the bear claw and relished the sugar rushing to her head. Was there anything more satisfying than a pastry? "We'll figure it out, we have to."

"I hope so. I'd be heartbroken if I had to close this place."

"Yeah, where else would I get bear claws like these? I don't know what you put in these, but they're addictive as hell."

"Sugar. And lots of butter."

* * *

"Morning, um, I'm the photographer for today," Andie said to the bored receptionist.

"You're early? Your agent isn't here yet."

"No, I know I'm early, I was wondering if I could talk to someone about a commercial rental property."

The weedy, thin man looked over his rectangular glasses at her and sighed. "You'd have to make an appointment. Obviously."

"I just had a few questions, that's all."

"You can make an appointment through the portal on the website."

"It would only take a minute. It's for a friend."

"Well, then, your *friend* can make an appointment."

Andie chewed the inside of her cheek. "I promised her that I'd ask for her, seeing as I already work here."

"You shouldn't have promised that without making an appointment." He glanced at the clock on the wall, then turned his glare back to Andie. "And according to your ID badge, you're a contractor, you don't work here. Not *really*."

"I'm here almost every day, of course I work here."

"My suggestion would be to request an appointment. Online. Through the portal."

"Fine," Andie muttered, whipping out her phone. "I'll just make one right now." She scrolled through the website, looking for the contact form. The man raised an eyebrow at her as she typed furiously, and then sent it.

His computer chimed softly. "It sounds like you have an email," Andie said smugly.

"We don't have any appointments today," he said, without looking at the schedule. "Bad luck."

"You didn't even look!"

"Because I, unlike you, do work here, and I know there are no appointments available until the new year."

"The new—listen, man, I'm not asking for the moon here. I just wanted to ask someone about a rent increase on a property."

The door opened and closed behind her. "Is there a problem here?" A woman asked, dressed in an expensively tailored skirt suit. "I'm supposed to collect a photographer before the open house today."

"Yes, that's me," Andie said, tugging on her camera bag. "I was just asking—"

"She wanted to make an appointment to discuss a commercial property, but I informed her that there were no appointments available."

"Well, which property was it? Maybe we can take a drive by it on the way to the job."

"The coffee shop on main."

The agent checked her phone. "That unit is currently occupied."

"No, I know, I just wanted to ask why their rent was being jacked up so high."

"Jacked up?" the agent asked, her blinding white smile almost painted on. "I think you'll find that we are simply bringing it in line with current market rates."

"But half the buildings on that street are empty. That coffee shop is one of the few things pulling in a profit!"

"With the speculative investors looking at those properties, it won't be long before the market rates increase alongside demand for those properties. We're just doing our jobs, it's not personal."

"It really doesn't seem fair to increase it that much in one fell swoop," Andie argued.

"Well, when you own a property, you'll be free to do with as you like, as is your right. It's the very essence of freedom."

Andie gawked at her. "You can't be serious."

"I am serious, yes."

"How is tearing away someone's dream freedom? You could at least give her more notice."

"If she doesn't want to lose her business, then she should consider branching out, selling some franchises, getting the branding out there."

"A business that small doesn't have the money for all that, not right now."

The agent shrugged. "Maybe she should consider finding some venture capitalists."

"Right. Well, I guess that answers my question. Should we head to the on-site location now, at least?"

"It's down by the reserve, for the new build there."

"Oh. I thought it was a property, given that the sheet said there was no lock box."

"It is, it just hasn't been built yet."

"But the new build is much further up," Andie said, reexamining the work schedule with a critical eye. She should have done it the day before, truth be told.

"No, that's the sport center and gym for the new build. The actual residences will be where part of the reserve is now."

"What?" Andie shouted, incredulous.

The agent stared at her with a quizzical expression. "Well, yes, that's all in the planning documents. The twenty new luxury condos will have access to their fully automated, twenty-four-hour gym and lap pool. I wish I was moving in there!"

Andie felt like the agent was trying to sell *her* one of the new condos. "What about the reserve?"

"Well, some of it will have to go, won't it? Fences can be rebuilt, and it's not as though a big empty plot of land is the city's best use of premium real estate."

"Since when is Applefield premium real estate? Have you looked around? There's nothing here!"

"That's what people want! A break from the everyday grind, to work from a balcony with a beautiful view instead of a high-rise office surrounded by smog." She gave another sparkling grin. "And it will be your job to make those spaces look as inviting as possible! That's why today, you'll be taking photos of what the view might look like."

"Is that before or after you bulldoze half the reserve?"

"Trees are trees, my dear. We don't need to be quite so prescriptive."

Andie shook her head. "I don't think it's right to be cutting down so much of the park. What about the animals that live there? I happen to know for a fact that some very rare plants can be found in that reserve..." She trailed off, thinking of Cat. No wonder she'd been so upset. She saw this coming a mile off.

"Are you going to come with me and do the job you were hired for, or not?"

"I just don't see how you people can sleep at night."

"Comfortably."

Anger burned in Andie's stomach. The *nerve* of it. "I don't think so," she said, her voice sounding far more sure than she really was. "I quit."

The receptionist snorted. "You can't quit, you're a contractor."

"I'm aware, thanks."

"And don't think you'll be eligible for unemployment, either. You ask me, you're giving up a great opportunity here."

"What, to grovel on my belly for scraps?" Andie sniped. "No thanks. You can all go straight to hell."

Before the door even slammed behind her, panic held her firmly in its grip. It was hard to pay rent from an empty bank account.

CHAPTER FOURTEEN

"Luke, what did you find at the county clerk's office?" Cat shouted down the hallway.

"We can enroll Dee from the start of the year," he answered through the closed door of the bedroom he shared with Felix, the yellowed white paint flaking at the rusted hinges.

"Good. Anything from the rental agent?"

"No. Might not hear until after the holidays." He opened the door, wearing his work uniform. "Any news about the development?"

Cat shook her head. "Unfortunately, no." The worry about where they'd shift, where they'd live, if the reserve got cut in half was becoming more pressing by the day.

"Mind giving me a lift? It's effing cold."

"Sure, I'll get my keys." She padded to the kitchen door and shoved her feet into her worn boots, shrugging on her thick parka, feeling glad that she'd had the foresight to take if off before that last shift. Coats were expensive to replace, especially now the fashion gurus had discovered thrift stores. "Ready?"

"Yeah. Closing shift tonight."

"I'll pick you up, just text. I don't want anyone walking home alone while poachers are still out there somewhere. Better to be safe than sorry."

"Can I come?" Delilah asked, standing in the doorway. "I promise I won't get in the way or anything."

"Hop in the back. I'm warning you, though, it's a boring trip."

"That's okay!" the teenager replied brightly, putting on the same clothes she'd worn in the woods.

Cat frowned, making a mental note to try to get the kid something else to wear. It was only going to get colder as the winter settled in, and no doubt she wanted something other than the boys' borrowed sweatpants on wash day. "Anita!" she shouted. "We're going!" When there was no response other than the muffled slamming of a door, she unbolted the door, taking off the chain lock, too.

They all piled into the truck, but Delilah looked absolutely thrilled to just be sitting in the back seat. "Seat belts, everyone," Cat announced, twisting the key in the ignition. The last thing any of them needed was to get pulled over for something as minor as a traffic violation. She didn't feel like explaining what a missing foster kid was doing in the backseat of her truck.

"Thanks for the ride," Luke said, scrolling through his phone, the screen cracked in several places.

"You know I'll always offer when I can."

"Got much work on tonight?"

"Eh." Cat shrugged. "Same old. Deliver some food, deliver some people. Might take a double shift tonight, make up some extra cash."

"I'd stay away from the reserve tonight, if I were you."

"Why?"

Luke looked out the window, tracing little designs in the fogged window. "I heard there's some kind of ground-breaking ceremony for the new build, or a party, or something."

"Assholes."

"Yeah." He leaned his head against the glass. "Do you think we'll have to move again?"

"Maybe. I don't see a way forward with five Bears running around in the woods every moon cycle." She saw Delilah in the rear-view mirror, looking concerned. "But it would have been the same problem with four Bears, too."

"And the newest one is just too cool to not have as part of the den, am I right, Cat?"

"Heck yeah you are!"

Delilah cracked a smile. "You don't have to say those nice things just because I'm here."

"We say them because we mean them. You have a place to stay, as long as you want it." Cat tapped on the gear stick. "You're a good kid, Dee."

"You coming in?" Luke asked as they pulled into the parking lot.

"Yeah. I wanted to—never mind."

Luke wiggled his eyebrows. "You wanted to see if Andie's been in, don't you?"

"Shut up. Don't tell Anita."

"Why, afraid she'll harass you about your double standards again?"

"Yeah, that's exactly why," Cat replied with a laugh. "I know I've been hard on you three over the years, but..."

"But this is different?" Luke finished.

"Okay, fine, you've made your point," she said, steering Delilah by the shoulders towards the door of the cafe. "Andie really is different, though."

"I'm just saying, don't be surprised if Anita starts bringing loads of boys back to the house."

"She'd better goddamn not, I need my beauty sleep."

Jazzy Java was bright, warm, and welcoming, just as it always was, but now, festooned with decorations to fit the season, and the scrumptious scents of cinnamon and chocolate drifting through the air. A hell of a lot better than the usual coffee smell that turned Cat's stomach, that was for sure.

"I'll text you when I'm done," Luke said, hanging his coat on a hook by the door and tying an apron around his waist. "Hey, Mara, is it okay if I gift my free shift drink to Delilah over here?"

"Of course!" Mara replied, popping up from behind the bar with a tray of freshly baked red velvet cupcakes with delicate green sprinkles strewn across the snowy white frosting. "What can I get you, sweetheart?"

Delilah's eyes were as big as saucers, reading the menu line by line. "I don't know," she said. "Everything sounds so wonderful."

"Take your time." Mara nodded at Cat. "I have something for you, but you'll have to give me a minute."

"For me? Has Andie been in?"

"She has, but you didn't hear that from me."

Cat felt a nervous little jolt in her stomach knowing that Andie had picked up the gifts Cat had left for her. Still, she hadn't texted yet. A bad sign. "Did you...?"

"Yes."

"And?"

"If you just take a seat in the squishy chair over there, I'll be right over." Mara raised an eyebrow at Delilah. "Do you know what you'd like?"

"Can I have the caramel eggnog gingerbread latte?"

"My personal favorite! Coming right up, little lady."

"That sounds terrible," Cat said with a laugh, sinking into the chair. "But I'm sure you'll love it."

"I've never been in a place like this."

"A coffee shop?"

"Yeah."

"Your foster parents never took you?"

Delilah sat in the adjacent chair. "They said caffeine would stunt my growth." She picked at her fingernails. "And then they kicked me out when I... when I shifted." The last part was said in a voice barely above a whisper.

"How much did they see?"

"Not much. Enough to start swearing up and down that I was a demon, sent by God."

Cat leaned over and squeezed Delilah's hand. "I'm sorry. That must have sucked."

"They never went to the papers or anything. I think they probably thought people would assume they were on drugs."

"That's usually what happens, yeah. But it's not fair that happened to you." Cat lowered her voice. "You're a Bear! You deserve better than some shitty foster parents!"

"I never really said thank you. For letting me stay."

"I wasn't about to turn you out on the street, what kind of monster would that make me?"

Delilah smirked. "If that's all it took to make a monster, then the world is full of them."

"Pff. Ain't that the goddamn truth."

"Okay," Mara said, emerging from the kitchen with a proud smile on her face. "I hope you both love this. Delilah, this is for you, and yes, the cookie comes with it. Fresh baked." She set the tall mug and accompanying cookie on the table next to her. "And this was a special request, but if it's good, we might decide to add it to the menu." She handed Cat a thick green mug topped with a veritable heap of marshmallows. "I was told that it had to be *the good stuff*. I hope it measures up."

Cat blew on the mug, feeling the warmth emanating through the ceramic meld into her skin. The smell of deep, rich chocolate wafted into the air. *Andie*, she thought with a grin. "Are you going to stand there and watch me?" she asked Mara, laughing.

"I need to see if it passes the test."

"Alright, alright." She brought the mug to her lips and inhaled, breathing deep the aroma that reminded her of safety and excitement. When the hot chocolate flooded into her mouth, she sighed contentedly. "Mara, this is the best thing I've ever tasted in my whole goddamn life."

"Yes!" Mara shouted, punching the air. "Alright, well, we need to add this to the menu, right?"

"If you want me to blow every cent I ever make in here, yes. This is delicious." Cat took another sip, savoring the flavor in her mouth. "Much better than that coffee crap."

"Speak for yourself," Delilah said, dunking the cookie into her latte. "I love this. Coffee is my new favorite thing."

"Come back when you're sixteen, I'll give you a job," Mara said with a wink. "There's nothing that thrills me more than coffee enthusiasts! And hot chocolate, now, too," she added. "Well, enjoy, ladies. I've got some stuff to finish up in the back, and I need to make sure Luke isn't burning tomorrow's muffins."

"I'm not!" he shouted from the back.

"So, you like it?" Cat asked, once she was alone with Delilah again.

"I *love* it. Thank you for bringing me."

"It's not always this eventful, just so you know. Usually it's just to drop off Luke and head back home."

"Do you really think she'd give me a job when I'm old enough?"

Cat shrugged. "Probably. But let's focus on getting you back into school first, yeah?"

"Deal."

"What do you want to be when you grow up?"

Delilah slurped at her drink. "I dunno. I like decorating things. Maybe something artsy."

An idea sparkled in Cat's mind. "That gives me an idea. Do you want to help me with a project?"

CHAPTER FIFTEEN

When Andie got home that evening, there was a tiny evergreen tree, with three spindly branches and wrapped up in a battery-powered string of lights, leaning against her door, blinking. She smiled and picked up the scraggly thing, carrying it inside and placing it in the window. There was a note with this one, too:

"A decoration, as promised. Don't know how long the batteries will last.

The hot chocolate was amazing.

I'm sorry, again.

–Cat"

She checked her phone, but there were no messages. Twirling it in her hand, Andie debated whether she should text Cat first. She was sorry, and besides, Andie quit her job with the development company. Seeing the stack of bills on her table made her stomach feel like she'd been eating rocks. It wouldn't be long before things were coming due, and there was barely enough in her account to pay for the next tank of gas.

Despite her financial woes, the thought of Cat at her door made Andie tingle with anticipation. The night they'd spent together just cuddling and watching movies had been one of the best evenings in recent memory for Andie, her arms around Cat as she slept, breathing deeply with calm reassurance. All she wanted for Christmas was more of that.

Cleaning out Daisy's cage, Andie hummed to herself along with the radio, that was playing the terrible mash-up remix Christmas song that she didn't quite want to admit she liked. She turned up the volume and sang to her chinchilla, who stared back, looking vaguely embarrassed. Andie responded by singing louder.

Setting Daisy back in her cage, she sat back and admired her work. "Not bad, right, Dais?" she asked, before belting out another tuneless chorus.

A knock at the door pulled her from her jam session, and she opened it to find a concerned looking Cat.

"Was that... you?"

"Was what me?"

"That... you know what, never mind."

"Singing? Yeah, that was me."

Cat kicked the snow off her boots onto the welcome mat. "It was very... enthusiastic."

"I like that song."

"That much is abundantly clear."

"Did you... want to come in?" Andie asked, opening the door wider.

"If that's okay."

"Of course, I was just thinking about you."

Cat raised an eyebrow.

"You know, because of the tree you left me," Andie gestured. "I love it."

"Delilah helped."

"Do you want something to drink? I have tea, coffee... wait, you don't like coffee. Er... there's some orange juice, maybe."

"I'm fine, thanks," Cat said, slipping off her boots and stopping by the cage to coo at Daisy. "I wasn't sure that I'd hear from you. I thought maybe you'd text, but when a few days went by, well, I assumed that might be it."

"I didn't hear from you, either," Andie said, standing in the kitchen with a tea, absorbing the warmth through the thick ceramic.

"I'm not very good at resolving things through text. I'm much better at creepily leaving gifts and hoping for the best."

"Well, I guess it worked. You're here now."

Cat nodded. "I saw that you put the tree in the window, and I went to the cafe earlier, so I thought maybe we might have a shot at this."

"Does Anita know you're here?"

"I'm sure she has some idea, given how aggressively she rolled her eyes at me as I left the house. She just finished the last of her exams, so she has more time to sit around and judge me." Cat sat at the table, wobbling on the stool, and poked the open camera bag that was sitting there. "New camera?"

"Rental, kind of. You're not allowed to smash this one."

Cat cringed. "I'm sorry about that."

"I know." Andie sipped her tea, savoring the peppermint flavor that flooded her mouth. "Please don't smash any more equipment, though. Shit's expensive."

"Andie, I—"

"Listen, I get it. You have a responsibility to your sister, and the boys, and now Delilah too now, I guess. I understand why you did it, but I'm still a little pissed off."

"Well, if we're airing grievances—"

Andie held her hand up to stop her. "If you're about to lay into me about my job again, don't bother. I quit."

"Wait, you quit? As in, your job?"

"Yes."

"For me?"

"For a variety of reasons. Fuckers."

Cat laughed so loud that Daisy barked at her through the metal grate of the cage. "So what are you going to do now?"

"Hell if I know."

"We should celebrate!"

"You want me to celebrate unemployment?" Andie asked, leaning against the peeling counter.

"I want us to celebrate your *freedom*."

"And how do you think we should do that? I'm fresh out of funds for a parade float or a champagne fountain."

Cat took her mug and set it down on the counter before wrapping her arms around Andie's neck. "Well, we could do this, for starters," she whispered, kissing Andie soft and gentle. "No one has ever quit a job for me before."

"Hang on," Andie said, pulling away with a sly smirk. "I just said, I didn't quit for you, I—"

"Shh," Cat hushed, kissing her again, running her hands up and down Andie's back, sending shivers down her spine. "I've spent every moment since I last saw you thinking about how to get you back."

"A text might have accelerated that process."

"It's been kind of busy at the house. Complicated."

"Is everything okay?"

"No, but it will be. You're here now, and that makes me happier."

Andie leaned into the embrace, burying her face in Cat's short cropped pixie cut. She smelled like figs and vanilla sugar, all sweet, with no spice. "Is there anything I can do to help?"

"Maybe. Not sure yet."

"Hey, even if Luke needs a ride to work, or Felix, I'm there."

Cat frowned. "But not my sister?"

"I don't think Anita would willingly get into a car with me at this point."

"She might, once she hears you quit."

"I guess we'll have to see about that. She's very... protective."

"She gets it from me." Cat kissed her again. "I'm very protective of the people I care about."

"Have you eaten?"

"No."

Andie cupped the side of Cat's neck with her palm and pulled her in for another kiss. "I can offer grilled cheese sandwiches and tomato soup. Zero of it homemade, unless you count spreading butter on bread the height of culinary excellence."

"That sounds perfect."

"And then maybe we can watch a movie, if you want?"

"Even better than perfect."

"We could just watch the same one as last time, seeing as you fell asleep fifteen minutes in." She opened her fridge and started to grab ingredients. "Or maybe not, if it was that boring."

"Let's watch something else."

"I've decided I don't like fighting with you."

Cat wound her arms around Andie's waist as she prepared the food. "I've decided that I agree with that sentiment." She rested her head against Andie's back. "So what are you going to do now, with your newfound freedom?"

"Hm." Andie wriggled out of her grasp to open the pantry door. "I don't know, really. I don't want to think about it. Too much stress. Money. Bills. It's all a pain in the ass, especially this time of year."

"Not going home for Christmas?"

"I don't want to talk about that either."

"Hey," Cat said in a soothing voice, "I'm sorry. I don't mean to stress you out." She looked around the kitchen. "What can I do to help?"

"There're some pellets over by Daisy's cage if you want to feed her dinner."

"I'd love to! I have to admit, I'm becoming surprisingly fond of that little mouse."

"She's a chinchilla!"

"It's basically a big mouse."

Andie laughed. "Don't say that too loud, you'll offend her."

The butter sizzled in the scratched nonstick pan, filling the kitchen with a tempting aroma. Cat rustled under the cage, pulling out the measuring cup and depositing food into Daisy's dish. Andie was surprised how... *normal*, it felt. As thought Cat had always been there as a part of her life, someone to come home to. She shook her head. She shouldn't get so attached so early on, especially not immediately following a big fight.

"Daisy, Daisy, give me your answer, do," Cat sang into the cage. "You're a little mousie, in a cage big enough for two!"

"Are you singing to my chinchilla?"

"She seems to prefer it to terrible Christmas mash-ups."

"No one ever accused Daisy of having taste." Andie leaned out of the kitchen nook and glared into the cage. "Traitor."

"You can't blame her for having ears, I mean, look at the size of those things! Massive!"

"You're one to talk."

"I sincerely hope you are not referring to my human form."

Andie flipped the sandwiches and stirred the soup, which was bubbling nicely. "Never."

"Though even as a Bear, I'll have you know my ears are perfectly proportioned."

"You are a very fetching Bear."

"I would eat you for breakfast."

"Promise?" Andie said, and immediately blushed a deep crimson. She pulled the neck of her sweatshirt over her head to hide her embarrassment. "I mean—uh."

"Let's focus on dinner first, shall we?" Cat asked, sweeping back into the kitchen, the hem of her sweater dress fluttering gently with the movement. "How is it looking?"

"Almost done."

Cat gently pulled the sweater back down. "You can't eat through that."

"No, I guess not," Andie agreed, pouring the soup into two large mugs and cutting the sandwiches in half. "Dinner is served." She set the mugs and plates on the warped table and slid onto one of the stools. "Might need some pepper."

"Mm," Cat agreed, reaching for the grinder. "Otherwise, it's perfect."

"It's just a grilled cheese."

"You didn't have to make it for me. You could have sent me home with an empty stomach. Hell, you didn't even have to let me in the door." She dipped a corner of the grilled cheese into the soup. "I probably wouldn't have."

"You're lucky that you're very cute."

"Is that the *only* reason you let me in?"

"No." Andie took a bite, enjoying the soft crunch of the toasted bread. "I missed you."

"I missed you, too."

"Did you expect this when you found me trespassing in the woods? Did you think after eating all my food that you'd... be eating all my food, again?"

Cat snorted. "That's not fair, I got dinner last time. I even bought cheap wine!"

"In fairness, had I known you were coming, I'd have bought wine, too - but someone doesn't believe in texting ahead."

"Oh, please. You love it."

Andie bit her lip. "I do." She took another bite, dunked in sweet tomato basil. "You make me forget my problems."

"That's weird, I was just thinking the same thing about you."

"Really? Despite being the thing you hate most?"

Cat blinked. "What?"

"A photographer."

"Hmm. I don't hate photographers, they just make life... difficult, sometimes. Things aren't always easy for Bears, you know. We've moved so much that I can't even remember all the places we've lived, trying to keep ahead of... well. Never mind."

Andie chewed the inside of her cheek. "Moving? You're moving?"

"I don't know yet, it depends on... a few things, actually."

"Oh."

"I don't want to. I'd rather stay here, have shifts in the reserve, spend time with you, let the others finish classes and apprenticeships, get Delilah back into school..." she trailed off.

"Well, I don't want you to go, either." Andie couldn't help but wonder what was bothering Cat, other than the obvious issue of the reserve being partially destroyed. She didn't know if she should pry or leave it alone, so she opted for the latter. "Are you done?"

"Yeah. Yes. Thank you, it was delicious," Cat said, stacking the dishes. "I'll wash up."

"Thanks. Soap is under the sink."

The television crackled with static as Andie flipped from one channel to the next, hunting for something to watch. She wished she had a modern TV, not this huge old clunky one she found at a second-hand furniture store for twenty bucks. Maybe a new one wouldn't be so prone to showing fuzzy channels until you smacked the side of it. "There's this one, if you want to watch it—" when she turned, she came face to face with Cat, who leaned in for a deep kiss.

"I really like you," Cat growled, slipping her hand under Andie's shirt, letting in a cold but refreshing gust of air. She kissed again, pressing past Andie's parted lips to explore her mouth with her tongue, breathing softly, sending jolts of electricity from her lips down between her thighs.

"I really like you too," Andie managed to say between kisses, her hands flirting with the hem of Cat's ribbed dress, clingy in all the right places.

Cat pressed up against her, pulling a gentle gasp from Andie's mouth. "I didn't think you'd let me in," she whispered, "but I'm glad you did."

"Mm." Andie traced her hands across the hem of the dress, sneaking underneath to run her fingers over the soft, insulated, fleece tights that Cat was wearing. It was like heaven, if there was one, a delicious temptation that made her heart race with excitement.

"I've never felt quite like this, you know."

"Me neither."

Cat tugged at the edge of Andie's sweatshirt. "Take this off."

"Okay." Andie obeyed, stripping down to her bra, vaguely embarrassed that it was her oldest, roughest looking one. She decided to take it off, too, before Cat noticed how decidedly un-sexy it was. "Now you."

"Fair's fair." Cat raised a playful eyebrow before pulling her dress off over her head, tossing it onto the bed, and pressing against Andie in just her tights and a purple lace bra that matched her hair.

Andie felt her pulse quicken, and wrapped her arm around Cat's waist, kissing her neck slowly, tracing the skin from her earlobe down to her collarbone. Cat moaned softly, urging Andie on.

Across the room, someone's phone started to vibrate.

"I should get that," Cat said, pulling away.

"Ignore it. If it's important, they'll leave a message or text."

"No, no, I have to see, you don't understand—" Cat wriggled from her grasp and bent to dig her phone out of her bag.

"Is everything okay?"

"I just need to make sure—" Cat stabbed at the green icon on her phone. "Hello? Anita? What's wrong—shit. Fuck. Okay, I'll be there as soon as I can. No, I'm not working, I'm—never mind. I'm on my way."

Andie was already putting her clothes back on. "Where do you need to be? I can drive you."

"No, it's okay, I have my truck."

"Can I help?"

"No," Cat said, sliding back into her dress. "It's probably best if you stayed out of it."

"Cat, if there's anything—"

"I said stay out of it, okay?" She gave Andie a quick peck on the cheek. "I'll let you know when it's all over."

"Should I call the police, or...?"

"Do *not* call the cops. We don't need them meddling in Bear issues, and they never help, anyway."

"Cat—"

The door slammed behind her, leaving Andie alone in her now very empty apartment.

CHAPTER SIXTEEN

Cat tried to keep her cool as she drove across town, despite the terror hitching her breath. Dee was missing, and some asshole reported a Bear sighting on social. It was already going viral, and it wouldn't be long before every poacher in three counties was heading to the reserve to bag a trophy.

Delilah must be having early shifts, maybe because she'd spent too long trying to hold them in. Cat should have suspected that might happen, should have warned the kid. She should have told the others to keep a closer watch on her. Instead, the poor girl was probably terrified, thinking something was wrong with her. The guilt burned in her stomach as Andie's kisses still burned on her skin. She shouldn't have been so careless. It was her fault that Delilah was in danger, after she'd promised to protect her.

"Goddamn it!" Cat shouted, smacking the steering wheel, the traffic light red. The truck's engine hummed in anticipation. Her phone vibrated again, and she pressed the speakerphone button. "What happened?"

"I don't know, she was in the back, and then all of a sudden she was gone! She's not answering her phone, but Felix put that location app on there, so we know she's in the reserve. Or at least, she *was*, until she turned her phone off."

"Why wasn't anyone watching her?" Even as she said it, Cat knew it was unfair. She hadn't been watching, either. She'd been screwing around with Andie.

"She was only in the yard!" Luke countered, emotion choking his voice. "I figured she'd be alright, I was making dinner, and then—"

"You're sure the sighting was her? No other Bears in the area?"

"They reported a juvenile bear."

"Fuck."

"I went outside right away, I was screaming for Dee, but she was gone." He swallowed audibly. "Her bag is still here. I think she might have run all the way there."

"Where are you now?"

"On our way to the reserve, Felix called a cab, but it's late."

"Where's Anita?"

"She took off running as soon as she realized what happened. At this rate, she might beat all of us to the reserve."

"I'll call you back." Cat hung up. "Call Anita." The line started to ring, and the light turned green. She gunned the truck across the intersection and passed a slow-moving car once she was on the other side. "Come on, Nita, pick up the phone."

There was no answer. The guilt in Cat's gut began to leech into her lungs, making it harder to breathe, the panic creeping up her spine vertebrae by vertebrae. "Answer, Goddamn it!" She called again. And again. No answer.

Cat was starting to envision her sister and Delilah both being shoved into the back of a van bound for some shadowy government basement laboratory just as she pulled into the old churchyard lot.

She leaped out of the truck and barely remembered to slam the door shut first, sprinting headlong down the path that led through the gap in the fence. There were no other cars around, did they go through the front gate? Had they signed in? It was unlikely, but there was nowhere else to park around here. Cat stopped in her tracks. Maybe that fucking ranger could help. She got back in her car and sped along the side street that led to the reserve entrance, tires squealing as she turned in. The lot was rammed full, highly unusual for such a cold night. In past years, snow on the ground tended to discourage the casual campers, but not this year. The goddamn twinkly lights the park staff had hung in the trees were pulling folks from hundreds of miles around. It was either tourists, or it was poachers. She swallowed hard, knowing how dangerous the latter was.

"Excuse me!" Ranger Dade was coming out of the building, clipboard in hand. "You need to sign in!"

"I need your help," Cat said, thrusting her ID at the ranger. "There are some bad people in the reserve, poachers—"

"You're the one who ran off a couple weeks back!"

"Yes, but—"

"Your background check returned some interesting results."

"Please, there's innocent people in the woods, a young girl, and I need your help to—"

"I think we should have a chat about your immediate ban from the reserve."

"Ranger Dade!" Cat shouted, her hands clenched into fists. "You can ban me for as long as you want, but help me get her back first!"

"Do you have proof of legal guardianship?"

"Jesus Christ, you really are useless, aren't you?"

The ranger frowned. "It's protocol, to protect against the misuse of ranger resources in the event of one parent or guardian trying to get another into trouble. We have enough problems in the park without getting involved in domestic disputes."

Cat's eyes filled with tears. "Please. I'm not her mother, and she's an orphan, a foster kid. I took her in because the place she ran from kicked her out for being different. They kicked her out, Dade! And now some tourist reported a bear, and there's going to be poachers crawling all over these woods shooting at anything that moves. Please, Dade. I know we haven't been on good terms, but I'm begging you."

The ranger dropped the clipboard to her side. "There are no bears in this reserve, I would know about it."

"I know that, but it's already going viral online. Everyone in a fifty-mile radius is going to be showing up here soon, looking for a bear."

"You realize I'll have to report this to child services. They might decide to send her back."

"It's better that than find her dead. Come on, Dade, please."

"Okay, then. Get in the ATV. Where was her last location?"

Cat was already running for the vehicle. "In the back nine, near where those big pine trees are."

"Let's go."

* * *

Andie pulled into the reserve in time to see Cat jumping into the ranger's ATV and speeding off into the woods. Well, at least she'd assumed right. Grabbing the camera bag from the passenger seat, she slung it around her shoulders and climbed out of her car, which was double parked in front of someone's RV. Hopefully they wouldn't be leaving until the morning. Hopefully she wouldn't come back to her car being towed.

She darted for the trail that led the deepest into the forest, camera in hand. She didn't know what was going on, but maybe if she got it on camera, it might help, especially if it was those poachers again. Assholes. Andie hoped they wound up in prison, sooner or later.

Her boots crunched on the wet, packed snow as she picked her way further into the trees, using the flashlight on her phone to light the way. Wherever the others were, it must be far from the trail head. She was regretting not sneaking in through the back. If Cat hadn't managed to pull the ranger away, Andie would have been stuck at the gate. Her stomach churned with anxiety, her lungs burning from the icy winter air. That asthma from her youth never had really cleared up, despite what the doctors had said about growing out of it.

The trail was empty, no hikers out this far or this late, choosing instead to stay by the cute lit walk at the entrance with the reindeer made out of tiny bulbs. She was alone and growing more terrified with every passing moment. Maybe she shouldn't have come. Maybe Cat was right.

Moonlight streamed through the trees, casting cold shadows after every bare tree, the twisting darkness reaching up for her with its spindly fingers. Andie stopped to listen, and heard nothing but the wind. *Damn it all to hell,* she thought. The reserve wasn't huge, but it was definitely large enough to get lost in, and she was quickly losing her way now that she'd left the path behind, her footsteps marred by the mud and leaves beneath, leaving no trace of where she'd been. A whole bunch of Bears in the woods, you'd think they'd be easier to find.

Wind rustled through the pine needles, the tops of the trees invisible amid the settling fog. The tripod smacked against the back of Andie's legs with every step, and the inevitable bruise it was creating continued to throb. She should have grabbed its strap as she ran out of the apartment, but she'd been so intent on following Cat to make sure she was okay that it hadn't crossed her mind until she was running through the parking lot. Now, there was probably an angry purple blotch on her thigh, but that would be the least of her problems if she got lost. Or ran into those poachers again.

She swallowed hard. This act of heroism wasn't going quite like she'd planned.

A few steps further and she was standing in that same clearing, blinking widely, willing her eyes to see more detail in the darkness. The full moon was beginning to rise, but the fog was dimming the brightest of the moon's beams, diffusing them into a smoky haze that played tricks on the mind. Was that someone in the brush, or just the gentle sway of some bushes? The glint of a flashlight, cutting through the thickly forested woods, or a trick of a desperate mind? At least she knew where she was now.

She shivered in the cold. It was already freezing, and dropping rapidly. There would be ice on the roads in the morning. She should have worn a thicker scarf.

Andie climbed into the nearby tree stand and buckled herself in, peering into the trees. The fog continued to descend, clipping the trees from view and making it even harder to see. Just as she was about to climb back down and continue her search, she heard voices in the darkness. Holding her camera steady, she began to record, despite not knowing where to focus the lens, and despite the on-board microphone being middling quality, at best.

"Where did you say it was last seen?" a man hissed. It sounded like the same one who threatened to shoot Andie out of the tree. She stiffened, trying to breathe as quietly as possible.

"Not far from here. It must be around somewhere."

"You have that dart ready?"

"Of course I have the goddamn dart ready, we're looking for a bear, not a raccoon." The second one huffed angrily. "*Do I have the dart ready.* Fuck's sake, man."

"Well last time you didn't, and we almost got our heads ripped off. Damn, I knew we saw a bear that night. All those assholes at the local will be eating their words now."

"Not if you don't have a way to prove it. Boss said no pictures, no nothing. Can't have any record of it or the hippie tree-huggers will be so far up our asses we won't be able to shit for months."

The first one shined a light into the trees. "Oh, I'm getting a photo of that thing once we bag it and tag it. They don't pay me enough to let this one go without a token."

"If the boss finds out—"

"Yeah? And who's gonna tell her, you? Fuck off, man."

"Will you shut up? I hear something."

Andie leaned as far forward as she dared in the tree stand, zooming in little by little on the far side of the clearing. A small Bear cowered in the shadows. The same Bear as last month, though considerably more filled out. Delilah.

The second one held some night vision goggles to his face, staring in the opposite direction, and Andie willed them not to see Delilah. "Man, this is stupid. I bet that bear already hightailed it out of here."

"What, and crossed through the local burger joint's parking lot? With all the eyes on this place right now, we'd hear about it. Besides, we don't get paid if some other dickhead bags it first. Won't matter that we've been out here almost every night for a month looking for it."

"At least we know we weren't crazy, seeing those two bears," the other one muttered, looking around. He turned to the other side of the clearing, and Andie's heart nearly stopped in her chest. "Shit! It's right here!"

"Well don't stand there with your jaw hanging open, shoot it!"

Andie unbuckled herself. "Hey!" she shouted, desperate to pull their attention. "Hey, assholes!"

"What the fuck? It's that goddamn photographer again!"

"Yeah, that's right, and I've got you on camera! What are you going to do now?"

"Same thing we meant to do last time," the second one said, aiming at her with the dart gun.

"Delilah! Run!" Andie screamed, but the Bear didn't move. Shit. Something must be wrong.

The first one walked towards the base of the tree. "You named it? You realize that thing could rip your face off if it wasn't caught in a trap, right?"

"You are scum, you know that?" Andie spat. "Fucking bear baiting? You're both so laughable, a fucking zombie couldn't find your brains."

"You'd be singing a different tune if one of these fuckers had chased *you* through the woods."

"One did, actually, but I'm not obsessed with the idea of killing something that's more powerful than me."

The second one laughed. "This is a job, babe. Maybe if you hadn't spent so much time in your liberal arts college learning how to take pretty pictures, you'd know what a real one looks like. Now come on down and let's talk." He aimed the gun again.

"No thanks, I'm okay, actually."

"I can just shoot you down, you know."

"I'll scream and bring people running. They'll find that poor creature in the trap you left there. Let her go, and we'll talk."

"Hell no, we aren't going to let it go."

Andie buckled herself back in. If they did shoot her, she didn't want to fall and break a leg, or worse, her skull. Where the hell was Cat and the others? She couldn't keep them distracted forever, sooner or later they'd climb up the tree to drag her down. "Pigeon-brained sheep fuckers!" she shouted. "You've got faces like three-day-old hamburgers in a parking lot! You couldn't find your way out of a paper bag, you snot-encrusted toads!"

"Yeah? Well, you're fat!"

"Is that the best you've got?" Andie shouted back with a snort. She could see a light dancing through the trees, and desperately hoped it wasn't more poachers. "Men have been calling women fat for so long, it barely even registers anymore." She followed the bouncing light, growing closer. "You complete fucking fucks."

"I'm going to need to see some kind of identification," Ranger Dade shouted, coming through the brush with a flashlight that lit up their faces. Poor Delilah looked terrified, shaking like a leaf. "We have reports of poaching in this area."

"We're not poachers. Now fuck off, we already signed your little clipboard."

"Craig? What are you doing with a gun? You're supposed to be here on Syndicorp survey business."

"Christ, I should have known the fucking ranger would show up. Listen, Dade, or whatever the hell your name is, this is much bigger than either of us, so I suggest you take a walk back the way you came, and pretend you never saw us."

"Firearms are prohibited in the reserve. I'm afraid I must ask you to leave."

"What about my God-given rights?"

"Sir. If you do not evacuate the park immediately, I will be forced to call the police."

Craig barked a laugh. "What do you think they're going to do? Do you even know how much Syndicorp donated to them this year?"

"That doesn't mean they'll overlook illegal activity."

"I think you'll find that's exactly what it means. Listen, Ranger, we're not trying to do anything crazy, alright? We just need to clear the reserve of bears and whatever the hell else is endangered so the ground-breaking doesn't get held up. We've got a schedule to keep, and a few pests aren't worth stalling progress, right?"

Ranger Dade rested her hand on her radio. "I never wanted you fucks in here to begin with. I went along with it, because my job depends on it. No Syndicorp money, no job." She glanced up into the tree, as though she was trying to make eye contact with Andie. "*If word got out about this*," she emphasized, "I think the company would have one hell of a public relations mess on its hands." She turned, seeing Delilah in the brush. "A bear trap? Really? Good God, I've met honest-to-Christ poachers who weren't this heartless."

Craig shrugged. "We had a job to do."

"You could have reported the bears to one of the rangers, we would have made sure they were safely relocated."

"That takes too long. Brings too much attention."

"Look around, Craig, half the goddamn forest is filling up with assholes just like you, looking for fifteen minutes of fame and a picture with a dead bear. You've got all the attention on this park that neither of us ever wanted." She bent and released the bear trap, her hand on Delilah's snout. "Don't bite me, okay?"

"Have you lost your mind?" the second one shouted. "That thing is going to kill us all!"

"It's a bear, not a machine gun," Dade snapped. "And to be honest, I'd probably let her eat you. You'd both deserve it."

"I don't think you understand what's going on here," Craig said, stepping so close to the ranger that they were almost nose to nose. "It's above your pay grade."

"I'm a Ranger, almost everything is above my pay grade. We don't show up to work every day, fighting with the county for scraps of budget and hauling drunk hikers out of the woods because we get paid well. We do it because we care about this godforsaken reserve, come hell or high water."

"It's fixing to become a flood, Dade."

Andie zoomed in on his face, the camera struggling to focus in the dark. A blurry silhouette would be better than nothing. Delilah still lay on the ground, whimpering softly, and Andie was wondering where the hell Cat was. Or the rest of the Bears, for that matter.

"Get the hell out of my park," the ranger said, her voice menacing. "And stay out."

"Your supervisor will hear about this, I promise you. We had a contract, and they're not going to want to see it fall through just because some bitchy rent-a-cop decided she'd rather have carnivores running wild. What will you do when one of those precious campers gets torn to shreds? What do you think will happen to this bear then? Or the whole damn reserve, for that matter?"

Ranger Dade rolled her eyes. "Bears aren't carnivores, you ignorant shit. And you know, I'm sure I will hear from the parks department, but I'll deal with that when it happens. Get. Out. Of my reserve." When the poachers hesitated, she poked Craig hard in the chest, sending him staggering. "If you're not out of this park in ten minutes—"

"What? What are you going to do?" Craig shouted, regaining his footing, hand on his gun. He spun around wildly, aiming his weapon out into the trees. Andie shrank back, trying to make herself as small as possible, and shroud her face in darkness. These guys didn't seem like the types to let something go, and she didn't want them trying to figure out who she was.

"I—" Ranger Dade stuttered, reaching for her radio.

"That radio isn't gonna help you now," he said, inching closer, finger on the trigger. "I came here to do a job, and by God, I'm going to do it." He stared into the trees, narrowing his eyes. "And don't think I won't be coming for you—"

A huge bear burst into the clearing, roaring so loud that the second poacher covered his ears in desperation. *Cat*, Andie thought excitedly, and all but jumped off her perch before she remembered that she should still be filming. A second, third, and fourth joined her, forming a circle around the injured Delilah. Cat huffed, and swiped at Craig. He held up his gun, but Ranger Dade knocked it from his hands. When he reached out for it, his fingers scrabbling through the frozen leaves, she kicked it into the bushes.

The Bears roared.

Goosebumps tingled across Andie's skin at the sound, the utter terrifying power they held. The second poacher had already fled into the woods, thwapping against hidden branches that scraped against the nylon of his waterproof parka. Craig kicked his legs out, trying to get away from the Bears. One of them, not Cat, snapped their teeth in the man's face, a hair's distance from his skin. He tripped over his own feet as he stood, turning for the path.

"I said, get out!" the ranger shouted, slinging the rifle's strap over her shoulder. "If I catch you in here again, I'll let them eat you!"

Craig didn't have much to say now. He scuttled into the night, and Andie watched until he disappeared into the trees.

"He's gone," Andie announced, unbuckling herself once again. Cat stared at her and nodded almost imperceptibly, so she stopped the recording and set the camera gently back into the bag around her shoulders.

"I hope that camera caught enough to raise a stink," Ranger Dade said, picking her clipboard up off the ground, dusting off the wet leaves. "Because if not, I'm going to be fired in the morning."

"Aren't you worried about the bears?" Andie asked, clinging to the climbing staples in the tree.

"They seem very tame, don't you think? Almost... human."

Andie froze. The poachers were gone, but now they had the park ranger to deal with. "Er..." she muttered.

"Almost seems a shame to send them to a zoo, or have them airdropped into a re-wilding area." The ranger turned and examined the Bears, who were still gathered around Delilah, who had begun to shiver in the icy wind.

"Is that really necessary? I mean, you could just let them stay—"

"There isn't enough room in this reserve for one bear, let alone five. I need to call this in immediately, before more poachers show up." She frowned. "This Syndicorp crap is really going to put a hitch in my budget next year. It's going to get harder and harder to patrol the forest with no money for staff or resources." She laid a hand on her radio again, and this time, Cat roared at her, knocking the radio to the ground. It was an oddly human behavior to see from something that looked very convincingly bear-shaped.

Ranger Dade squinted. "Just as I thought. *Bears.* Well, that certainly explains a lot, doesn't it?"

"Explains what?" Andie prompted, still clinging to the ladder. She wanted the ranger to think she was afraid of the Bears, not taking one of them out for coffee and a romantic hike up to the falls.

"Maybe you should head back to the front gate. I imagine you have some editing to do, before you get that footage into someone's hands?"

"What about the bears?"

"I wouldn't worry about them. I assure you, they wouldn't want to do anything to *draw attention to themselves,* at least any more than they already have."

"Er—"

Cat stepped back into the brush, the wet sounds of skin reforming and bones popping. "Alright, let's cut the crap, Dade."

"I should have known the sightings were goddamn *Weres*. Shouldn't you be out west somewhere? Not in the middle of a small reserve in the middle of the Midwest, for chrissakes?"

"It's complicated."

"*Bears*. I knew I smelled something rotten."

"Oh, please. We have a much better sense of smell than you."

Ranger Dade scoffed. "I doubt that." She cast a glance toward Andie, who had finished climbing down from the tree stand. "What about her, then?"

"She's fine, don't you worry about her," Cat said, stepping out of the brush, tugging her boot on, her dress covered in nettles and branches. "Goddamnit, I really liked this dress."

"What are you, an amateur?"

"Why don't you just mind your own business, and we'll get out of your hair?"

"Are you serious? Every poacher in a hundred miles is parking up here to get their hands on what they think are genuine bears. Do you have any idea how much trouble you've just dumped on my plate?"

"That photographer up there is my girlfriend." When she said it, Andie's stomach fluttered. *Girlfriend.* "And I brought her here, and she has the footage that's going to save all our asses, not to mention the goddamn forest, so give me a minute, Dade." She squinted. "Fucking Wolves," she muttered.

"Hang on, the ranger is a Werewolf?" Andie barked, laughing.

"Keep your voice down," Dade hissed. "Some of us actually want to keep that hidden, instead of parading around through public property like some kind of lawless exhibitionist."

"Oh, please, as if Wolves haven't been posing for photos in Yellowstone for years. No one would even know about Wolves if you canines hadn't been so reckless."

"Reckless? I'm not the one—"

"I don't have time for this. We need to get her home."

"What was she even doing, shifting before a moon?"

"She's young still. Spent months trying not to shift after her foster parents kicked her out."

The ranger softened. "That poor girl."

The other Bears wandered back into the brush, one at a time, emerging in rumpled clothing. Felix laid a huge fleece blanket over Delilah and patted her head gently. "You should shift back if you can, Dee. We need to get that ankle seen to."

"She needs to calm down first," Dade said, putting her own thick coat over the top of the blanket. "And warm up."

"What about the other poachers?" Andie asked, worried more would show up that they wouldn't be able to scare off. Poachers with bigger guns.

"I'll fend off what I can," Dade said, "but you should get her the hell out of here." She tossed the keys to Cat. "Take the ATV. *Don't* let anyone see you, and I goddamn mean that."

"We can't just take her through the front gate, there's no way we won't be seen."

"I'll move the truck to the churchyard," Luke said, fishing Cat's keys out of her coat pocket before tossing it to her. "Let's go."

CHAPTER SEVENTEEN

Cat tossed another log into the fireplace and sat next to Delilah, still a Bear. "You'll be alright," she said softly, tugging another blanket off the couch to drape over her. "It's okay. We're all okay."

"She's shivering," Andie said, standing in the doorway.

"It's normal for Bears to shiver when they get too cold, just like humans. She'll warm up soon. I think the early shift and that damn trap scared her. She'll shift back when she's ready."

"I'm just glad she's safe," Felix said, perching on the edge of the couch with a mug of coffee. Cat wrinkled her nose at the acrid smell.

"I don't know how you can drink that stuff."

"Because it's delicious, obviously. Andie, you want some? There's a fresh pot in the kitchen."

Andie ran a hand through her hair. "Yeah, I would, actually. Been a hell of a night."

"We just have to hope that Ranger Dade holds up her end once the footage goes wide," Anita said. "If she pulls back and says it's a hoax, or that the video is edited or whatever, we might not be able to pull this off. Although," she said, smirking at Andie as she reentered the room with a steaming mug, "this was my idea from the beginning, but Cat would have no part of it."

"That was different!" Cat retorted.

"Oh please, it's exactly the damn same. I'm just glad I finally got my way, for once." She tossed a cookie to Andie, who snatched it out of the air. "Nice one, Andie. It's a good thing Cat asked you to follow us into the woods tonight."

"Er... yeah," Andie said, sipping her coffee. "So long as everyone is safe."

"When is that footage going to go out?" Luke asked, setting a few apples in front of Delilah. At first, she seemed disinterested, but then started to snaffle them one by one. "We probably shouldn't waste any time."

"Already done. I hopped on Cat's laptop while you were getting Delilah settled, I sent it to a journalist friend of mine. She was more than happy to take the scoop. I bet we see things start hitting by sunrise. Mercy hadn't answered a phone call in weeks, but she's a good connection to have."

"Yeah, well, fingers crossed people get as outraged as they should, and get that new complex canceled," Cat muttered.

"That's right, you *work* for them, don't you, Andie?" Anita asked, her tone barbed enough to make Cat wince. "Surprised to see you on our side of the fence, then."

"I quit."

"Really?"

"Yup. Lying bastards. I'll bet half the county board who approved that monstrosity didn't even know how far in it was going to go. They intentionally obscured the property lines in their presentation. Nothing technically illegal, but it's sure as hell unethical. We just need people to agree, call the board, demand they take back the contract. It will probably cost the city a pretty penny to get out of it, though."

"There's already a crowdfunder posted," Felix said, flashing his phone screen to the rest of the room. "It's called Save the Applefield bears."

Cat snorted. "They can save us by just giving us that stack of cash."

"Looks like they want to buy back some more land around the reserve, like out by that churchyard, and re-wild it. Make the park bigger, expand it."

"Well I'll be goddamned," Anita said appreciatively. "This might just be the best possible outcome."

Delilah swallowed the last apple and stretched out beneath the blankets.

She'd shift back soon. Cat scooted back to give her more space and motioned for the rest of them to turn around. Poor kid didn't need an audience, not after tonight. A shift sounded like a zipper made of bone, a dry, crunching sound, with the delicate echo of skin stretching over newly formed muscle.

It's why they were so goddamned tired after shifts. She could already feel herself getting sleepy, despite the abbreviated time that evening as a Bear.

"You're okay," Cat said again once Delilah finished shifting back into her human form. She wrapped the blankets tight around the girl and gave her a hug. "How are you feeling?"

"I'm so sorry!" Delilah sobbed, bursting into tears. "I didn't even think, I thought I could just go and come right back, I should have said—"

"Hey, shh, it's alright. Everyone in this room—" she looked at Andie. "Well, almost everyone in this room anyway, has dealt with this at some point. It's totally normal. You'll gain more control as you get older. You have no reason to feel ashamed or guilty."

"But if someone had gotten hurt—"

"We didn't. And even if we had, we were there because we care about you and want you to be safe. Now, let's have a look at that ankle, okay?"

Delilah nodded, sniffling, holding the blankets tightly around herself, like a cute little Bear cocoon. Cat was so grateful that she was safe. She'd never have forgiven herself if something worse had happened. As it was, the kid was probably going to be traumatized for a while. Delilah stuck her foot out from under the blankets, hiccuping and sniffling. It was black and blue, and swollen as hell. Cat frowned.

"Can you wiggle your toes for me?"

Delilah nodded and crunched her toes inward before stretching them back out.

"Any tingling?"

She shook her head. "No."

Cat looked at one side, and then the other. Lateral and medial malleolus intact, no obvious signs of breakage. That much was good. "Can you put weight on it?"

"Kind of. It hurts, though."

"The punctures aren't too deep. Felix, can you grab me some gauze from the first aid kit in my bag?"

"Do you think it's broken?"

"I think it's a bad sprain, Dee. You're going to have to rest up, okay? You should be alright tomorrow."

Andie coughed into her coffee. "Tomorrow? After she got caught in a damn bear trap?"

"We heal quickly, especially if it's an injury we get while shifted, and then shift back."

"What, so you're like, immortal?"

Cat furrowed her brow. "Of course not. But we can take more of a beating than humans can. One of the few perks of being Were." She turned back to Delilah and squeezed her shoulder through the thick blanket. "You should get cleaned up. One of the boys will make you some food. How does tuna casserole sound?"

"Yes, please," Delilah said, a smile spreading across her face for the first time that night.

"Do you want me or Nita to help you?"

The girl stood up, resting her weight on her uninjured foot. "I'll be okay by myself. It's already feeling a little better."

"You can use my fancy bubble bath if you want," Cat whispered theatrically. "It's under the loose board in the cabinet."

"So that's where you hid the good stuff," Anita grumbled.

"Yes, because you were using it all!"

Anita scoffed, and then grinned. "Well I know where it is, now."

"I'll hide it somewhere else," Cat retorted. "Boys, do you want to get started on some food? We're all about five minutes from ravenous hunger." As they squeezed past Andie in the doorway, Cat's eyes fell on her hips, and something within her stirred. "Andie, do you mind giving me a lift to your place? I think I forgot something there. I don't want to leave them without the truck."

Andie bit her lip and smiled. "Of course."

* * *

"I don't know what you left here, we both flew out of here in such a rush," Andie said, pushing open the door to her apartment.

Cat's body was like a coiled spring. Odd, as an off-cycle shift usually left her feeling sluggish and headachey. The slight sleepiness she'd felt at home had dried up in the icy winter air. "Oh, just my scarf," she lied. She just wanted to be alone with Andie again. After tonight, she needed some peace. Delilah would be safe with the others. It wouldn't be too long before sunrise, anyway.

"There's some random stuff in the fridge, if you're hungry. I'd offer takeout, but I'm like, super broke until I find some other work."

"I'm okay." She'd eat whatever the rest of them had left when she got home.

"I'm covered in mud, I'm going to jump in the shower."

"Sure."

Andie stripped off her soaked hoodie and tossed it into a laundry basket by the door. Her t-shirt was clinging to her breasts, scrunched up at the hem and showing just a peek of pale skin. Cat's heart skipped a beat.

"I'm happy to drive you back when I get out."

"Mm," Cat murmured. She didn't want to go home, not yet.

"That was pretty wild tonight, huh?" Andie said, stepping into the bathroom. She left the door ajar enough for Cat to see her clothes dropping to the tile floor, one article at a time. Cat pressed her hand against the door, wishing she was on the other side of it.

"Mhmm. You really saved my ass tonight, Zanetti."

"I wasn't about to let you go into the lion's den without some backup." Andie snorted. "Lion's den. For Bears. Hey, are there WereLions?"

"Yes. I've never met one, though.

"What Weres *have* you met?"

"Bears, mostly. A few Wolves. A Jaguar once, named Micah. He was cool." The sound of water trickled under the door. "Andie, would you—never mind, actually."

"No, what's up?"

"It's nothing. Forget it." A blush began at the base of Cat's neck and started to creep towards her face. It was stupid to even ask.

Andie poked her face out the cracked door. "I literally ran into the woods and climbed into a tree stand tonight for you, I doubt anything you need is going to be more intense than that."

"I was just wondering if I could shower here. There's five of us at the house now, and we all share a bathroom, and—"

"Of course you can."

"Oh."

"I won't be long."

The thought of Andie naked behind that door made Cat's pulse quicken. "We could save water. Shower together." Even as she said it, she cringed inwardly. *Get it together, Cat,* she thought, looking down at the threadbare hallway rug.

"I like the water as hot as it goes."

"Me too."

Andie pulled the door open another inch. "Come in, then, you're letting all the steam out, and it's cold as hell outside tonight."

"I heard it might snow."

"Yeah."

Stop talking about the weather, you absolute nerd, Cat thought, still looking down at the floor as she closed the door behind her. If she looked up, her brain might explode right out of her skull - though it wasn't really her brain she was thinking with right then.

"Are you planning on showering fully clothed?" Andie asked.

"No." Cat hung her jacket on the towel rack and fumbled with the zips on her boots, finally kicking them off next to the white canvas hamper in the corner. She still didn't have the courage to raise her gaze up from the floor. Then, in an instant, Andie was there, pressing herself against the fabric of her dress, pulling up the hem past the waistband of her tights, unhooking her bra.

"Is this okay?" Andie asked, kissing Cat on the neck so gently, she wanted to cry.

"Better than okay."

And then, all at once, they were both stepping into the avocado green tub, the stream of piping hot water covering them both, sending tendrils of mud down the drain. "Soap," Andie said, handing her a bottle of body wash that smelled like pine and peppermint.

Cat poured some into her palm, lathering it generously before spreading it across Andie's chest and down over her hips, tracing her fingers over the curves of her body almost reverently. When Andie reached out and cupped Cat's hip bone in her hand, she let out the tiniest of gasps.

Andie soaped up Cat's body slowly and methodically, letting every speck of dirt rinse away until they were both clean. Cat turned around and let Andie massage the shampoo into her hair, letting herself melt into the moment and feel at ease for the first time ever. She was safe here, in this protected bubble, warm under the hot water that turned their skin pink with the heat, allowing herself to lean back into Andie's embrace as she coated her hair with conditioner.

Then, Cat did the same for Andie, and then they were standing in the heat, their hands on each other, exploring every curve, kissing across bare skin and tracing invisible patterns across the sparkling droplets of water that lingered there.

"Should we...?" Cat whispered, pulling Andie closer.

"The hot water is going to run out soon."

"I guess it's good we shared, then."

Andie stepped out, squeezing the water from her hair. She grabbed a fluffy towel from the rack and leaned over the rim of the tub to wrap Cat in it, rubbing her hands over the terrycloth fabric to dry her before taking another towel for herself. "Fuck, it's cold," she said, laughing. "Race you to the bed?"

"Hell yes." Cat shook the water from her short pixie cut hair, sending droplets across the bathroom. She tousled her hair with the towel, keeping as much of it wrapped around her as possible. That draft from under the door was damn icy. She'd be surprised if it didn't snow. They both ran from the bathroom to the bed, leaping beneath the heavy blankets and reaching for the warmth of the other.

"So what now?" Andie asked, but before the words were out, Cat was already ducking her head beneath the covers, her hands on smooth skin, her lips covering every inch of Andie in sweet, soft kisses. It was bliss, an enveloped, impenetrable bubble of calm. Whatever was going on outside, it didn't matter. Cat pulled her legs underneath her to keep under the safety of the blankets, still kissing softly, zig zagging across the velvet skin of Andie's stomach.

When she reached the dense thatch at the meeting of her thighs, Cat eagerly kissed, and teased, and caressed. She pressed with her fingers, gently exploring, drawing a gasp from Andie. She pressed further, and faster, still kissing, until Andie was gasping for breath, her fingers clutching Cat's shoulders.

"Come here," Andie said, breathless. "I want to see you."

When Cat emerged from the blankets, Andie pulled her into a deep, slow kiss, her hands pulling at Cat's hips until she was able to tease at her entrance. Cat moaned softly, leaning into the touch, driving Andie deeper inside, pressing at the most sensitive part of her. It was the most alive she'd ever felt, like energy was pulsing through every cell in her body, jolts of pleasure building a heat at her core. She ground her hips against Andie, her head thrown back, her breathing quickening, letting soft cries of satisfaction slip past her lips until she was rocked with the uncomplicated joy of it, the finality that was really only a beginning.

When she lay next to Andie, encircled in her arms, she almost wanted to cry with the overwhelming emotions. She snuggled closer, burying her face in Andie's chest.

"Can I ask you a question?" Andie asked.

"Yes."

"Did you mean what you said at the reserve, when you called me your girlfriend?"

Cat looked up at her. "If you want that to be true, then it is," she admitted. "I'd be crushed if you sent me on my way now. Not after *that*."

"Hell, no," Andie growled, pulling her closer. "You're not going anywhere."

* * *

Andie climbed out of her car with a wide, exaggerated yawn. She wished she was still in bed. "Are you sure that we have to meet them *today*?"

"That's what Anita said," Cat replied, slamming the passenger side door. "I mean, it would be nice if this was all over."

The old truck tore into the parking lot, despite the dusting of fresh snow across the recently paved road. Anita jumped out, waving at them, while the others climbed out of the cab. "Hey!" she shouted.

"I told you not to drive like that," Cat warned, but she was grinning ear to ear.

"Lighten up, Sis, today is a day we *celebrate*."

"It's not every day the city council decides to have an emergency, in-person meeting this close to Christmas," Felix agreed. "They must be backing out of the contract."

"Wouldn't that just be the best Christmas present?" Delilah asked, still limping slightly, but leaning on Luke.

Anita nodded. "It would be unbelievable."

"Are you here for the meeting?" a harried assistant asked, standing with the door wide open. "They're just finishing up."

"What? They told us ten in the morning!"

"Yes, for the open session. Their closed session with the legal team began at seven." They ushered the group in, tucking a stray lock of platinum blond hair behind their ear. "Now, if you'll just follow me, it's right through here."

"I don't know if this feels good, or bad," Cat whispered into Andie's ear. "It really feels like it could go either way." She interlaced her fingers with Andie's and squeezed gently.

"It's going to be fine, I bet," Andie replied.

"Hello, hello, please come in," one of the council members said, a grumpy looking man in a bright green elf hat like he'd been yanked straight out of a festive party that had gone on into the wee hours of the morning. "I'm sure we'd much rather all get this over with and get back to... whatever we were doing." He cleared his throat and gestured for them to sit down. "I know you may all be wondering why we asked you here this morning, this very *early* morning," he said, casting a sideways glance at one of the other members. "After the footage at Pine Meadows Reserve garnered attention from local and regional media outlets, it seems as though last night's events went *viral*."

"Sorry to interrupt, I just wanted to ask if anyone wanted anything to drink," the assistant said, a notebook in their hand.

"Lou, forget the drinks, we want to make this short and sweet. I know you want to get home to your family, too. Just collect their paperwork, if you don't mind. Thank you." As Lou backed out of the room, the council member continued. "As I was saying, it's become clear that Syndicorp was caught violating certain terms of the contract with regard to flora and fauna preservation. This story is gaining traction, but they wish to… change the narrative, so to speak."

"We're listening," Cat said, leaning forward in her chair.

"Syndicorp has offered you all a modest cash settlement to keep your words out of the press. We know that Ms. Zanetti's footage is where much of this is coming from." He turned and looked at Andie. "Your friend at the paper wasn't shy in extolling your many talents as a photographer."

"How modest is modest?" Anita asked.

Lou came back in with crisp white envelopes, all sealed from end to end, each with one of their names scrawled across in green ink. They set the envelopes on the table and perched on the nearby stool. "Please, take your envelopes. If you wish to accept, you will be asked to sign a simple agreement."

"And if we don't accept?"

"Then we would reach out to Syndicorp's legal team."

Andie tore hers open, and her heart jumped into her throat. It was enough to pay her rent for a whole goddamn year. "I can't take the footage down, not really, it's all over the internet by now." Annoyingly, most outlets had used her footage without her consent or paying her.

"No need." The councilman slid a stack of contracts across the desk. "I can also say, Ms. Zanetti, that the local paper is looking for a regional photographer. It's my understanding they have their door wide open for you, should you be interested. As for the reserve, we've become aware that a crowdfunding effort has taken off, and while nothing will be finalized until the new year, it looks like it will not only be keeping the area previously let to Syndicorp, but it will be doubling its size. We're to understand that Ranger Dade over there is undertaking major efforts for conservation and tourism, and to build out the existing camping pitches. As such, we will be allotting a much larger portion of the city's budget to the park, and we will be needing some help. We are in need of on-site nursing staff on a flexible, rotating schedule with two others, as well as a graphic designer and laboring work, electrics, you know, the works."

"So basically, you're bribing us," Anita said slowly. "To not go to the press with what we know about Syndicorp. Even though the story broke last night."

"They are hoping that without further media coverage, the story will die down considerably."

"What are they going to do, head to the next place with a nice view and set up shop there?" Anita shook her head. "It's bullshit."

"The plans for this particular development have been put on hold indefinitely. They may decide to go in another direction entirely, as most reserves and parks won't want them within ten miles. They've also sold their commercial properties in town back to an independent community fund."

Luke snorted. "Good."

"That means the cafe is safe," Andie said, pulling out her phone to text Mara.

Anita looked in her envelope again, and then back at her sister. "This could really change things for us," she whispered. "And you get to be a nurse."

"Fuck it," Cat said, wiping a tear from her eye and snatching the papers from the desk. "Merry Christmas to us."

* * *

Money couldn't buy happiness, but it sure as hell helped. When Andie sat down at the table on Christmas day, she nearly cried tears of joy. Food, piled so high you could barely see who was sitting across from you. Laughter, joking, and the best goddamn turkey she'd ever eaten. Felix said the secret was a three-day brine with aromatics. All Andie knew was that she'd be sneaking over more often when he was cooking. Cat rested her hand on Andie's knee beneath the table, giving her a gentle squeeze of reassurance every now and then.

"It's time for presents!" Anita squealed, skidding across the faded linoleum tiles in her fluffy socks.

"When did you get time to go shopping? We were only not broke as of yesterday morning!" Cat called after her with a laugh.

"I'm efficient! Come on!"

They all piled into the living room, while Andie stacked the dishes in the sink. "You too," Cat said, pulling her gently.

"Okay, first present goes to Delilah, because she's the youngest," Anita declared, tossing a shallow box tied with a bright green bow. "This is from the Bears."

Delilah eagerly tore at the paper, tossing the top of the box aside. "Bear pajamas," she said, her eyes welling up with tears.

"We filed the rest of the paperwork on the way home yesterday," Cat said. "We have to wait until after the holidays, but it looks like we'll be your official guardians."

Luke stood proudly in the doorway with another box. "This one is from me and Felix," he said, handing it over. "Sorry it's not wrapped."

"Caramel syrup!" Delilah said, laughing. "My favorite! Thank you!" She wiped her tears with the back of her sleeve. "Thank you, all of you. I don't know how I got so lucky."

"Good things come to good people," Anita said, beaming. "Andie, we got you something, too."

"For me?" Andie took the box and shook it gently.

"Just open it!"

She tore at the glittery tape at the seams of the paper, exposing the crisp white box underneath. It smelled like a department store, and when she pushed aside the crunchy tissue paper, she raised an eyebrow. "Koala pajamas?"

"Yeah. Not a real bear, but everyone sort of associates them with bears, anyway. We thought it kind of fit."

"Does that mean I'm allowed to date your sister?"

Anita rolled her eyes. "Please. It's not like Cat ever listens to what I say anyhow. But, yes. If you're asking for my blessing, you've got it. You really went to bat for us, Andie. We don't forget stuff like that."

"Welcome to the den, Andie," Felix said with a grin. "We hope you'll stick around."

"I'm not going anywhere," Andie replied, wrapping her arms around Cat.

"You're all stuck with me, now."

Epilogue

Andie hung the photograph on the wall opposite the door in her apartment, straightening it gently.

"I'm proud of you," Cat said, wrapping her arms around her waist. "It's a beautiful picture."

"I've already had emails from magazines asking me how the hell I managed to get a photo of five bears playing in a blizzard in December."

Cat shrugged. "It was fun. I suppose now you'll be wanting to take trips to parks all over the place to photograph other wildlife."

"Mm," Andie nodded, leaning back into the embrace. "I'd like it if you came with me, though."

"I'll put a time off request in at work. If you wait until spring, I'll have some paid time off banked."

"Consider it done." Andie squinted out the window at the bright night sky, and the moon rising over the horizon. "It's almost time," she said. "Did you want a lift to the reserve?"

"Nah. Tired." Cat released her and slipped her dress over her head, folding it over a hanger on the back of the door. "Think Daisy will mind?"

"She's asleep."

Andie turned the lights off, smiling at the gentle flickering Christmas lights she still hadn't taken down, even a month later. She put a video of a fireplace on the television, and set a huge bowl of apples on the floor, atop the new plush rug she'd bought.

When the huge Bear lumbered over and flopped down on the rug, Andie snuggled against it with a happy sigh, giggling at the soft snaffling sounds as it crunched through the apples. They were her favorite. For once, everything was going to be okay.

About the Author

First, I have to thank my wife, whose tireless enthusiasm and encouragement are what push me back to writing even on days I feel like I never want to write another word again.

Another huge thanks to my Sunday morning writing group, without which I'd sleep until noon on the weekends and never hit word count.

And finally, I want to thank YOU, the reader, for using your precious time to read this book. I hope you will join me in my steampunk sapphic space pirate series, The Cricket Chronicles, out now.

You can connect with me on:
- https://ryannfletcher.com
- https://twitter.com/IMRyannFletcher
- https://facebook.com/RyannFletcherWrites
- https://instagram.com/RyannFletcherWrites

Subscribe to my newsletter:
- http://eepurl.com/gOQBaP

Also by Ryann Fletcher

The Cricket Chronicles, out now, is a sapphic steampunk space pirate series.

 **Deus Ex Mechanic, Cricket Chronicles book 1**
Alice is the best mechanic the corrupt Coalition regime has ever seen. When she's kidnapped by an infamous vigilante space pirate named Violet, she has to make the hardest decision she's ever made: escape back to the comfort of the Coalition, or risk everything to fight injustice?

When Violet decided to ransack Coalition vessels, she never though she'd have to fight her feelings for Alice, too. Will giving into an affair with the treasonous mechanic cloud her judgment and jeopardize the safety of her crew?

As they fight side by side against ruthless rival pirate captain Leo and his crew, will they grow closer together, or will everything fall apart and leave them stranded in dark space?